THE MASTER'S VOICE

BY
ZAK JANE KEIR

ISBN 978-1-0815-0562-2

AUTHOR'S NOTE

The Master's Voice was originally written more than 10 years ago, and the short stories, mostly, not very long afterwards. While some bits have been given a slight polish, I haven't updated them much, so the tech-savvy might notice that all the references to online BDSM antics, and communications technology in general, are less than contemporary.

Look on it as an illustration of how much and how fast the world has changed, if you want.

CONTENTS

CHAPTER ONE

Bramble cables sank sharp thorns into the tender flesh of her thighs, and a branch whipped across her face, stinging her cheek. She fought free of the hostile plantlife, her skimpy black PVC raincoat coming unfastened and flapping open in the howling wind. She was naked underneath it, but there was no one around to see her as she struggled up the overgrown, slippery pavement.

The house was built on the side of a hill, a huge great place, probably dating from the late 19th century, and the road leading to it was in a fair state of disrepair, presumably to deter casual callers. She wasn't worried about cars, she was keeping to the paving only so as not to break an ankle or something on the potholed road surface: falling and being unable to get up would be an incredibly stupid move, and probably wreck everything. She had only been out in the rain for a matter of minutes, but already she was drenched, and cold. She didn't bother to retie the coat or even pull it round her, just let it flap loosely around her slender body. Now the time had come, she was actually there, actually doing it, she hardly noticed the physical discomfort. Finally, she was at the bottom of the stone steps which led up to the solid, squared-off porch and the heavy, studded oak door. She shook her chin-length, silver-blonde hair out of her face, stumbling a little in her high-heeled, shiny, black, ankle boots, and made her way up to the top. Up above was a wild sky, clouds hurtling through the darkness, only intermittent gleams from the waning moon. The wind was roaring in the trees. She couldn't have picked a more dramatically appropriate night if she'd tried, she thought, and almost laughed, then shuddered. There was a lot at stake here, more than she'd been able to admit to anyone, even herself. She lifted the big iron cobra's head knocker and knocked.

~

When he opened the door, he was wearing a black, velvet, fur-collared robe and holding a glass of brandy. He was a short, bald man, broad-shouldered, dark-eyed, with a neatly-trimmed goatee beard, and he exuded menace. She'd told herself, and others, that he was absurd, just a poseur, but she'd known deep down and undeniably that he was more than that, and here was the reckoning. For an instant, she thought he was taken utterly by surprise but, if so, he rapidly gained control over it. She'd hoped to catch him at least slightly unawares, yet one of the things she couldn't have known was just how surprised he might be. She hadn't, right up until the last minute, been sure if it would be better or worse if he treated her arrival as something routine. She stepped into the hall and he looked her up and down, raising one eyebrow in a calculated, mannered move he couldn't quite hold as his face involuntarily broke into a wide, exultant grin, and she felt a little better.

~

'Well, Malorie?' he asked, as she stood on the threshold, shivering, legs bleeding in a couple of places from the bramble scratches, soaked from the rain.

'I had to come.' She tried to pull the coat closed around herself, then let her hands fall. 'You called me, you've been calling me for weeks, I know you have. I couldn't deny it. I had to come.' Her heart was pounding, her pussy damp, partly from excitement at her own daring, partly from a nasty, squirmy, dirty little touch of genuine arousal. Would he laugh at her, would he throw her straight out of the house? Or would he believe her?

He threw the brandy glass away; she heard it shatter on the flagstone floor, and then he was on her, one hand tangled in her silvery hair, pulling her head back as the other hand snatched the coat off her, leaving her naked but for her shoes. He slapped her face, hard, forehand then backhand, and she gasped.

'You want to be mine.' It wasn't a question, but she nodded, or tried to, her hair still held painfully tight. Abruptly, he let her hair go and she staggered a little.

'Go to your knees,' he said, and she obeyed. She thought he would command her to suck his cock, but when he opened his black velvet robe the thing was limp and flaccid. Before she had managed to formulate, much less articulate, anything that might have broken the moment, he was pissing in her face, over her windblown but lovely hair and over her breasts. 'Lesson one, cunt.' he said. 'Everything has to be earned.'

~

They probably could have parked the car a bit nearer but, firstly, neither of them wanted to blow it by having any of the neighbours spot them, or by being captured by any of the hidden cameras that just might be attached to the trees up and down the private road at the top of which the house squatted, in classic sinister fashion, widely spaced from its fellows. Also, the layby nearest the turning, though sometimes an impromptu doggers' site, was going to be deserted on a night as classically dark and stormy as this, and Ricky and Malorie needed one more fuck. Well, perhaps not a fuck.

'I can't go to him with your come in me, can I? He'll smell it, or something.'

'He wouldn't care. Or he'd think it was even more proof of his fucking powers, wouldn't he? That you'd just get straight out of bed and come running over to his place in the middle of the night. But I don't have to come in you. I can come in my hand, or your hand, or my pants. I don't have to come at all. But I want you one more time. If you're really going to do it, girl.' Ricky paused for a moment. He couldn't help hoping she'd change her mind, yet he knew she wouldn't.

'You need it too, don't you?' he said. 'One more before you go. Let me lick you out, let me take the taste of you away with me.'

Malorie, in her black PVC raincoat, nothing underneath it, arched her back and thrust her tits forward, licking her lips. 'Are you begging, baby? Are you going to beg me?' She grabbed his hand, pulling it across the gap between the seats and opening her legs so his fingers brushed the little strip of hair that decorated her pussy. 'Can you make me wet, can you earn it?'

Ricky moved forward, leaning past the wheel, kissed her on the mouth, hard and deep, wanting to turn the car round right now and take her home, no matter what they'd said and agreed, no matter how important this was to her. They were halfway to the middle of bloody nowhere, in the middle of the night in an area with crappy mobile reception... She wasn't even taking her phone: how would she get help if it all went wrong in the first few minutes? She broke the kiss, stroked his face.

'Into the back,' she said. 'In the back, and you'll service me on your knees'. That imperious tone was creeping into her voice, and it made his cock stiffen and throb.

They opened their doors, shut them, opened the back doors, slid into opposite sides of the car. Now Ricky could kneel behind the passenger seat as Malorie leant back against the other door, drawing one leg up, parting her thighs so he could get at her hot, wet sex. He buried his face in her, licking and sucking, plunging his tongue in and out as she twisted her fingers in his hair, pulling just hard enough to turn him on even more as he drank her juices and tongued her clit, hearing her breathing speed up and feeling her body jerk and tremble, and then she squealed and gave a little sigh and her pussy seemed to melt into glorious wet warmth as her hands tightened on his head. She let him go and he straightened up, aware that he had just come in his pants, his nose full of the scent of her, sweet juices drenching his blond moustache.

'Bitch. I love you.'

'I love you, too. It'll be all right. I promise it will.'

Then she had put her boots back on and got out of the car, and he'd watched her walk away into the storm, and he'd wanted to go after her and grab her by the coat collar, haul her back to the car, throw her over the bonnet and beat her with his belt until she came again. Instead he'd waited until she was out of sight, and then he'd put the battered old Vauxhall back in gear and driven home.

~

For authenticity, Malorie thought, he should have dragged or thrown or ordered her down a long, cold, dark flight of damp stone steps, but he merely opened the door to the right of the big central staircase and gestured her into a gloomy corridor. Perhaps the house didn't have cellars, after all: no one had ever actually mentioned them. She noticed, briefly, that there was another door off to the left of it, and a mezzanine floor with two archways above: the whole thing like some kind of church or theatre, and the high roof of the hallway crying out for bats and chandeliers.

'Crawl, cunt,' he said, and Malorie obeyed. About six feet along was another door, opening into what was obviously the house dungeon. It could have been the playroom in any half-decent fetish club, its walls black, its floor concrete, assorted heavy, solid items of fetish furniture standing in a vague circle, and a rack of whips and crops and floggers and other implements bolted to the furthest wall from the door. Next to this implement rack was a doorway, and she couldn't tell whether or not there was any kind of light coming from it, the torture room being only illuminated by wall sconces with nightlight bulbs. As his hand closed on her hair again and he lifted her and put her over a lightly-padded whipping block, she thought she heard a female voice raised in a question or cry of alarm, but couldn't be sure.

'I'm going to beat you,' he said. 'You might think you have a safeword. You might still think there's a universal safeword. But it depends how much you want to belong to me, doesn't it?'

Malorie licked her lips, suddenly feeling genuinely afraid. 'I – I want to belong to you, Master,' she ventured, and without any warning he shoved her off the whipping block so that she fell hard onto the stone floor. She yelped in pain, aware of grazes on both knees and one elbow.

'I know you do, cunt,' he said. 'All cunts want to be owned by a real Master. It's just that most of them won't admit it. And when they do, they wonder why most real Masters don't want them. But what I want, I take. You tried to resist me, and you couldn't, and now you're going to learn what it's really all about. Get up and bend over that block.'

She got up, a little clumsily, wondering if she should ask for permission to take the damn ankle boots off, deciding almost instantly against it. She bent over the block, thighs apart, buttocks raised, balancing precariously on her toes, reaching down to grasp the thing's legs. One hard, heavy smack landed on the left cheek of her arse; she felt the strength in him and shuddered.

~

After that first smack, the Master paused for a moment, letting his eyes roam over the girl as she waited for his next move. He warned himself, silently, not to rush things, not spoil the future opportunities by being too greedy with the present one, but oh, the temptation she presented. He was serenely assured of the success of his Method, if properly used: apply the right stimulus to the right cunt and she could be taken, trained, owned and – even more pleasingly – shown off as proof that what he said was true. He had wanted Malorie Jackson for some time now, his desire for her increasing the more she snubbed him or mocked him: he had known, of course, that once he put his method to work he would be able to take her from that useless blond oaf she lived with – lived with! The idiot hadn't collared her, or married her, they just 'lived together'. Ricky Smith had no idea of how to assert himself and put a female in her proper place: he actually boasted about his 'relationship' with Malorie being based on switching. Switches, as far as the Master was concerned, were idiots, lying to themselves, though not as much as allegedly dominant women lied to themselves. Men who claimed to switch were simply inadequate, trying to appeal to women by pretending to show a softer side: men who were submissive were failures. He dismissed them all, mentally. That Malorie had never shown the Master any respect in the past was annoying but also arousing, he had known it would make her eventual surrender all the sweeter. That Ricky showed him no respect was irritating, but irrelevant in the long run. It still made it extra satisfactory to have used the Method on Ricky Smith's woman and to have called her to his home, into his possession. Now what mattered was to break her, and break her fast, reduce her to a screaming, begging, crying, wreck. She'd accept it. But she had to learn who was in charge, and learn it straight away. He took a heavy-duty rubber flogger from the rack and set to work at once, thrashing her shoulders and upper back till they glowed red and she was whimpering.

'Stand up,' he commanded, stepping back. 'Face me.' She did as she was told, hanging her head so her silvery blond hair fell forward, hiding her expression. Her hands and arms were trembling; she made a move as though to clasp her hands behind her back, but didn't complete it. He drew the strands of the flogger through his fingers, then abruptly lashed it across her breasts, once, twice, then a third time. She squealed, and staggered from foot to foot.

'Stand still, cunt.'

She was breathing hard, but not crying yet, though little moans escaped her. He went to the implement rack, hung up the flogger and selected a thick kooboo cane. She raised her head as he passed in front of her, flexing the cane, and he saw her eyes widen in fear. It pleased him some more.

'Touch your toes.'

She wanted to refuse, he could tell. She knew how much that cane would hurt, especially on an arse given almost nothing in the way of a warm-up. He almost wished she would refuse, because then he would throw her back over the whipping block, and this time he would cuff her hands to it so she couldn't escape – but how much sweeter and more brutal it was to make her bend and take it, unsupported. Trembling badly, she bent over, wobbling a little, but managing to steady herself, the tips of her slender fingers pressing against the shiny black toes of her stiletto boots.

The first stroke of the vicious cane brought a shriek from her, and he laid five more on in rapid succession, relishing the whoosh and crack as her screams rose in volume each time. Six bright white lines appeared on her arse, the surrounding skin flushing red, and then the welts deepening and darkening. Her hands moved on the sixth stroke, and she tried to straighten up, so he hit her with a seventh, harder than the rest, then goosed her roughly, more of a push than a grope so that her balance went and she tumbled to the floor on hands and knees. With his bare foot, he pushed her over onto her abused back, and spat into her sobbing, anguished face. She rolled again, screaming a little, rolled on her side away from him and curled up, crying. He turned away, and called in the direction of the arched doorway that led inwards:

'Helen! Come out, cunt. Look after the new cunt. She's come to join you.'

Without bothering to wait and see if this order was obeyed, he left the room, a fierce exultant grin on his face and his cock now standing proud. In his office on the first floor, he could watch anything that happened, in either the dungeon or this anteroom, by means of a couple of closed-circuit cameras which fed to a pair of tv screens. He sat in his leather swivel chair, stroking himself as the first bitch interacted with the new bitch. He would begin other necessary procedures when the time was right, using delay switches where necessary. When he orgasmed, it would be without ejaculation, the better to conserve himself and his energies for the next day.

~

Malorie couldn't stop crying for several minutes. She had expected pain, of course, she had been prepared for humiliation, but she hadn't expected to feel so helpless, so soon. Was it really worth it? She thought for a moment about getting out, right now: if the door was locked she could damn well smash a window, climb out of it and run, find a phone box and call

Ricky to come and get her – but what good would it do? If the police got involved, they would probably say she'd asked for it, and so would a lot of people, and nothing would be achieved.

She struggled to get herself under control as it dawned on her that she wasn't alone in the dungeon. She heard movement, and then a hand touched her shoulder, tentatively, finding one of the few places that wasn't hurting. She shrieked and jerked away, then opened her eyes and looked up into a worried, pale, female face. It was one she recognised: the slave girl she had seen with the Master on several occasions.

'It's OK, OK,' the girl was murmuring. 'He won't come back in here tonight. Can you get up?'

Malorie gulped, and rubbed her hand over her face, swiping away the tears. 'Yes. I think so.'

As the other girl, a petite, curvy brunette, stood up, Malorie carefully got to her feet and followed the stranger through the doorway furthest from the entrance hall. A low-wattage bulb hanging from the ceiling gave just enough light for her to see that this room was almost bare apart from a double airbed on the floor topped with a tangle of rough-looking blankets. Crooning reassuringly, the other girl led her to the airbed and helped her to lie down on her side: Malorie's arse hurt far too much for her to try to sit. The girl quickly but gently pulled Malorie's boots off and set them at the foot of the bed.

'My name's Helen,' the girl said. 'Poor you, that sounded awful. But the first night's always bad. You have to want to submit to him, really want it, and then it doesn't hurt so much, you can bear it more. But he knows what he's doing, he really does.' Her voice was soft but high-pitched, somehow quite soothing and, as she talked, she was stroking Malorie's hair and arms, steering clear of anywhere the marks of either flogger or cane were with a sure gentleness. Malorie no longer wanted to cry, but she still felt shivery, and after a while Helen lay down, drawing the blankets up over them both and then starting to pet and soothe Malorie again. She supposed it wasn't that surprising that Helen lived with the Master, though it hadn't figured in Malorie's plans: still, the other girl was at least not inclined to be hostile towards her so far. She didn't seem particularly surprised by Malorie's arrival, either, and Malorie wondered what she actually felt about it. Perhaps she would find out.

'Have you been with him long?' she asked the slave girl, once she felt she had her voice under control. Helen nodded. 'A few months.' Then she smiled, which Malorie found a little unnerving. 'It's all worth it. It really is. He's like nothing you've ever had before. You'll see.' Helen kissed her on the forehead, and one of her hands moved slowly, tentatively down over Malorie's whipped and throbbing breasts. Malorie drew in a shaky breath, feeling a sudden wash of arousal through her body. For sex of some sort to follow a beating was nothing new as far as Malorie was concerned, but she hadn't expected either to want it or to get it tonight. She slid her own hand over Helen's hip, up the other girl's body, and Helen pressed against her more closely. Malorie tensed briefly, expecting more pain, but it didn't happen, and she could feel that the agony of the whipping was beginning to shift into that deep, glowing warmth she sometimes craved – and got – when Ricky thrashed her. Right now, she would take any comfort she could get, and this girl, with her gentle touch and soft voice, was thoroughly comforting. The previous times Malorie had seen her, Helen had been in the role of absolute, abject submissive: crawling naked on the floor, forbidden to speak. To have the girl direct their encounter, assert herself, however gently, made Malorie feel first glad, then confused. Was Helen another enemy, or a potential friend? The only thing to do, really, the only possible thing to do, was to take her as she seemed, for now.

'Yes, it'll help,' Helen murmured. 'You're so pretty, mmm, and I can make you feel better.' Her leg slid slowly in between Malorie's thighs, and Malorie bent her head so she could take one of Helen's nipples in her mouth. The other girl's breasts were big, soft and full, and the nipple erected against Malorie's tongue as Helen moaned, caressing Malorie's smaller tits in turn. She trailed her fingertips down Malorie's belly, then slipped her hand between her legs, cupping Malorie's smooth-shaved quim. Still licking Helen's nipple, Malorie felt for Helen's pussy, enjoying the springy softness of the other girl's abundant muff-hair, feeling the labia, how hot and wet they were. Her own pussy was rapidly juicing up again as Helen's index and middle fingers dove inside it and began to pump in and out. Malorie matched her rhythm, finger-fucking Helen's snatch, using her thumb to strum the other's clitoris. Helen came first, legs clamping on Malorie's wrist as her sex clenched on Malorie's fingers, but she kept her own hand moving, moving, and Malorie felt her whole body tingle and shudder, her pussy spasming hard in a fast, strong orgasm that took almost all the pain out of her caned-raw bottom and assorted scrapes and wounds.

'We'll suffer tomorrow,' Helen whispered when she'd licked her fingers clean. 'We're not supposed to come unless he tells us to. But he likes us to disobey him sometimes, I think.'

As far as Malorie could tell, Helen fell asleep within seconds of her final sentence: Malorie herself expected to lie awake for some time, but quite suddenly she found exhaustion overwhelming her. She tried to think of Ricky as she slipped into unconsciousness, pictured his face for a moment, his hands, his cock. Then there was nothing but blankness, for a while.

~

The Master gave a low groan of satisfaction and took his hand from his softening penis. No mess, of course: he was master of his own body. He pushed a couple of buttons to start the audio programmes, then got to his feet, turning his back on the viewing screens. Time for some sleep now. Tomorrow was going to be an interesting day. The conquest of Helen had been satisfying, but hardly a challenge: Malorie was a far more interesting prospect. He had summoned her, and she had appeared, undoubtedly the first of many who would demonstrate the effectiveness and the truth of his Method. He decided, there and then, that he would take Helen's training to another level: he had been on the verge of growing bored with her, but the arrival of Malorie opened up further avenues of possibility.

CHAPTER TWO

Rumours about the Master had been permeating the scene for some time before Ricky and Malorie first encountered him. People said that there was this guy who no woman could resist, who had an empire of subbie girls who would do anything he wanted, that he was dangerous and to be avoided, that he was terrifying, that he was irresistible, that he was a well-known lifestyle dom that no one had ever heard of, that he was going to make everyone sit up and take notice... But rumours were just rumours. Malorie and Ricky were used to rumours, liked hearing them, sometimes liked to help circulate them, more often than not helped to step on them when the rumours were ludicrous, unfounded, or outright spiteful. They'd been running Thrillers, their fetish and adult goods shop, for three years now, having decided to do it within weeks of meeting. Ricky sometimes said the idea had come to him shortly after their first explosive sex session, that he'd known straight away that the two of them belonged together and should pool their resources as soon as possible, and though Malorie sometimes implied that the initial idea had in fact been hers, she wasn't particularly bothered about who had thought of it: it worked and that was enough. Both of them had been trading for a while at the various fetish fairs and markets before they ever properly met, to supplement wages earned in boring, unimportant day jobs. They'd been doing it, separately, long enough almost to make a living from it: both had a finger on the pulse and a knack of getting people to tell them things. Thrillers had become a hub for the scene within days of opening, and they had felt almost as though they had some kind of cosmic good luck alchemy on their side.

It was Malorie who'd come up with the name, giggling at the almost-synchronicity of their own names: Ricky and Malorie, Natural Born Thrillers. They'd had t-shirts made on their third date, a trip to the seaside out of season, when they'd dared each other to strip and jump into the freezing sea. Then it had been a mutually enjoyable battle of wills as to who was going to get out of the water first: Ricky had conceded when he saw her lips turn blue, and the spanking she gave him under the pier had soon boosted both their circulations enough for an uncomfortable but ecstatic fast screw on the sea-drenched pebbles, right there with the waves hissing up within feet of them. He was on top by that time, pounding into her slick wet pussy, holding her shoulders down, biting her neck – the way they could both switch roles mid-scene, mid fuck was one of the strongest links between them. That this infuriated some of the kinky people they encountered didn't bother them: those who were most determined to insist that Malorie and Ricky were somehow 'faking it' were the ones who came into Thrillers most often, presumably in the hope of somehow catching them out, though neither Ricky nor Malorie knew or cared what the idiots might be looking for. The idiots nearly always spent some money, no matter how annoyed they got.

Gossip and speculation and other people's prurience wouldn't have kept them afloat if the shop hadn't been a good one, though. Before they took the plunge and tied their professional and personal lives together, Malorie had been a clothing trader, not bothered about making things herself but with a sharp eye for what was good and a logical charm that persuaded the innovative and new-on-the-scene designers that she could sell their wares better than they could themselves. Ricky was the leather craftsman and occasional gadget-maker, technically accomplished with just enough originality to keep customers interested. As both of them were connoisseurs of filthy literature, they'd added a range of quality erotica to their collective stockpiles when they opened, and their separate and joined network of scene contacts meant that all the hobbyists and perfectionists and part-time traders were happy to supply them with an assortment of interesting goods. It was as though they'd moved to another level, made a public commitment to the fetish lifestyle as much as to one another. They now went to the fetish markets only to catch up and check out what was new, though they did as much of that when they went to the clubs. Neither of them could be all that bothered with the various online message boards and discussion groups that catered to the kinky and recreational sex communities, though Malorie occasionally liked to log in and, as she put it, pull a few tails.

She had seen a few comments about The Master and his female slave training methods, some hostile, some approving, most just idly speculative, and both she and Ricky had heard his playing style discussed. The concepts of total domination and enslavement were not exactly new, and most people seemed to wander around the idea of letting others do what they wanted as long as it was safe, sane and consensual, with a persistent minority arguing in favour of consensual total non-consent and, Malorie sometimes said to Ricky, threatening to disappear up their own jacksies in an effort never to judge anyone else. If The Master had a proper name, no one seemed to know it. He was, apparently, very wealthy, but how his wealth had been acquired was another mystery. Some had heard that his father was some kind of pharmaceutical ace involved in creating and marketing new medicines; others insisted that The Master made his money from teaching other would-be dominant males how to proceed. There was also talk of him being involved in electronics and new media technology: what all seemed to agree on was that he had a definite persona and presence, and something of a following among those who favoured male-dom-fem-sub kinkiness. He was, apparently, often to be seen in the clubs, but seemed not to stay too long in any one place.

~

On this particular night, in late spring, Malorie and Ricky had both been in a mood to enjoy some public fun but had not got around to choosing or assigning roles for each other before they went out. They were both, therefore, dressed in what they considered fetish-neutral: Ricky in black leather jeans and boots and a t-shirt he'd stashed in the cloakroom on arrival, Malorie in a violet satin boned corset that left her pert breasts bare, violet fishnet hold-up stockings, black PVC ankle boots and a short, flared, black rubber skirt. Sometimes, they went out in clearly role-defined clothing: Malorie in next to nothing, Ricky in either full leather or a tuxedo – or Ricky in little more than collar, cuffs and black leather shorts, Malorie covered up in second-skin-tight rubber or leather, gloved and maybe even masked. Sometimes they could give their outing even more of a charge by choosing, part way through the evening, to switch roles at the toss of a coin so that, costume notwithstanding, the dom became the sub and vice versa. But, more often than not, they simply dressed in whatever they found sexy and agreed to let the night happen in whatever way it would.

Tonight, they were at Unforgiven, a longstanding favourite club of theirs and one which had weathered about eight years of ups and downs and fetish scene politics, including two or three changes of venue. Its current homeplace was a below-street-level and thus atmospheric City pub which generally shut on the other three Saturday nights of the month. Ricky and Malorie had secured a pair of stools at the far end of the long mahogany bar, well-placed to survey the room, but far enough away from the speakers over the miniscule dancefloor to be able to talk, and to listen.

Where the bar ended and a couple of half-arches divided the cellar into what was, in the venue's daytime incarnation the drinking and dining areas, black drapery had been used to make the division clearer: behind this was where the dungeon space existed. Malorie and Ricky had taken a peek in there earlier and seen only three or four single men loitering hopefully near the St Andrew's Cross, and a couple whose demeanour suggested it was their first-ever club visit, giggling to each other as they sat side by side on the black leather-upholstered rack. There would probably be more action fairly soon, but the Natural Born Thrillers were happy to wait, and watch, and listen to what was going on.

~

Ricky saw him first: a short, stocky man with a shaven head and satanic-style goatee, accompanied by a naked girl on a lead, on all fours. Presumably the girl had disrobed on arrival: Ricky had a mildly amusing mental snapshot of her master waiting patiently outside the ladies' loo while she got out of whatever clothes she'd travelled in. The man was moving swiftly through the crowd towards the bar, and people were getting out of his way, probably in order not to inadvertently tread on the girl's hands as she crawled along on her lead. He wasn't taking much care of her, Ricky thought, just ploughing on ahead, not looking down at her, hauling on the lead until he got to the bar and set his elbows on it. 'Brandy,' he said, curtly but not rudely, the tone of someone who expected to be obeyed without question. 'Double brandy.' He was swiftly served, and swiftly moved away: Malorie, who had been talking to Dizzy, who made props and dungeon furniture for a lot of the clubs, noticed the bald man's departure and sniffed derisively. 'Bit overdone, don't you think? And it's a good job for that poor cow that the smoking ban came in, otherwise she'd have fag burns all over her knees by now.'

'Oh, don't be so mundane, darling.' Dizzy sighed. 'There's a certain style to it, after all. It's hard work being Mr Utterly Eeeeevil, don't you think?' Malorie shrugged. 'Yeah, OK. Maybe when they get home, he's busy washing the dishes while she sits and watches Sex and The City all day. Whatever.'

Malorie had a clear, carrying voice and it just so happened that the music playing quietened temporarily as the DJ changed tracks: the bald man clearly overheard Malorie's remark and directed a look of contemptuous outrage at her. Malorie smiled sweetly, wiggled her fingertips in a derisive wave and returned her attention to her drink.

~

The night progressed; the dungeon livened up. Ricky became embroiled in a detailed and technical discussion with Dizzy about suspension cuffs, so Malorie spent some time on the dancefloor, enjoying the various lecherous looks her performance garnered. The DJ tonight was one of those who wasn't afraid to be eclectic, mixing Britpop and industrial and punk classics with well-chosen chart selections. At the end of a joyous, sweaty work out to The Gossip, Malorie noticed a tall, well-built redhead eyeing her appreciatively and gave her a wave. Natasha Williams, who was tonight wearing head-to-foot scarlet latex, a simple domino eyemask, tightly boned and laced corset, long panelled skirt, matching gloves and spike heeled boots, was a deliciously inventive dominatrix with great style and a sense of humour. Both Ricky and Malorie were equally happy to bend over at the touch of her whip or have dinner with her and one of her handful of willing slaves. She seemed unaccompanied tonight, but Malorie couldn't imagine she'd stay that way for long unless she wanted to.

Malorie's dancefloor session went on for quite some time, but eventually she grew tired and thirsty. She headed back to the bar, availed herself of a bottle of Becks and wandered into the dungeon in search of Ricky. She was starting to feel horny, in a bitchy kind of way, and wondered how the mood of the night was taking him. She could envisage tying him to one of the items of dungeon furniture and teasing him for a good long time, maybe jacking herself off in front of him but just out of his reach, maybe blindfolding him and using a spiked metal wheel all over his body...

In the dungeon, two or three scenes were in progress, but next to the currently-unused A-frame, Natasha was in conversation with the short, shaven-headed man. His slave knelt at his feet, head bowed, not participating in the exchange at all, which was not that unusual. However, Natasha looked more put out than Malorie ever remembered seeing her, so naturally Malorie drifted into listening distance.

'That's why you're not happy,' Baldy was saying, with a condescending grin. 'Because what you really need is to meet a man who can master you. Women don't handle power well. They need to be owned, it's just that feminism and all that bullshit has made them afraid to admit it.'

'Steady on, matey,' Malorie put in, with the sudden realisation that this had to be the Master people were talking about: that he was not, after all, a myth dreamed up by the more fevered members of the online fetish community, as she and Ricky had been beginning to suspect. 'What happened to respecting other people's kinks? There's plenty of girls who want a dominant man, but not all of them do, so take the stick out of your arse and get on with topping the girls who want it.'

The Master looked at Malorie, and when she met his dark eyes, she felt a little, visceral shiver. 'Another one who's lying to herself,' he remarked. 'When you have the courage to admit what you really need, you'll come to me. Or someone like me.'

'I've got what I need, thanks,' Malorie said.

'So have I,' said Natasha, reaching out with one hand to feel underneath Malorie's skirt and give her bare buttocks a friendly squeeze. 'And the people who haven't got what they want yet will find it for themselves sooner or later. '

The Master raised his brandy glass to his lips, drank deeply and then tossed the glass in the direction of his slave girl, who caught it and held it quietly. 'Sooner or later, you'll admit it,' he said. 'But you'll only get to belong to Me if you're worth having.' Turning away, he gave a jerk on the slave's lead: she put the glass to her mouth and gripped the rim with her teeth before starting to crawl away. The Master steered her with the lead, moving at a measured pace, his head high, clearly enjoying the speed with which people got out of his way.

Ricky reappeared at that point, putting his arm across Malorie's shoulders and kissing her lightly.

'Having fun yet?'

Malorie put her hand up to his chest and pinched his right nipple, quite hard. 'I could be about to,' she said. 'Get on your knees.'

'Hey, Natasha,' Ricky said, not obeying instantly. 'All right? That shortarse bothering you, was he?'

'She told you to get on your knees,' Natasha stated, with an imperious lift of her eyebrow. 'Didn't she?'

Ricky glanced from one to the other of the women, then went down in one easy, sinuous movement to kneel at Malorie's feet. He bowed his head, waiting, and Malorie exhaled. She knew that, if Ricky really hadn't been feeling subby, he'd have let her know without making a squabble out of it; she also knew that he wouldn't be at all averse to letting Natasha join in any scene Malorie might begin. It wouldn't be the first time. Natasha, eyebrow still raised, looked at Malorie, who smiled and tangled her fingers in Ricky's blond hair.

'I think he's been a bad boy,' she said. 'Bad enough for both of us – if you're not otherwise engaged, right now?'

~

Helen, the Master's slave, knew that the Master was angry with the two women who had sneered at him, and that his anger was about to be taken out on her. She felt a delicious but slightly queasy thrill of anticipation run through her body as she made her way to the bar on hands and knees, the brandy glass held firmly in her mouth

'Up,' the Master commanded, jerking on her lead, and she raised herself to a sit-and-beg position, enabling him to take the empty glass from her and set it on the bar counter. He didn't speak again, merely tugged the lead and set off back towards the dungeon, and she hurriedly got back down into the crawl position in order to follow him.

The dungeon was busy: Helen could tell from the number of pairs of legs moving hurriedly out of the way as the Master dragged her through the doorway and off to the side. Into view came a solid wooden base with a post at each side and she had to come to a halt to avoid bumping into the thing. The Master gave her lead an upwards tug, then another one, and she got a little unsteadily to her feet. He had brought her to a set of stocks and, still without speaking, he lifted the upper bar and snapped his fingers. Helen bent over, placing her head and hands in the appropriate half-circles, and the Master lowered the bar into place and slid the bolts that fastened it shut. Helen began to tremble, aware of the Master pacing around her. The stocks held her head still so that, though her eye level was higher up than when she had been crawling, she still couldn't really see what was going on. The Master passed in front of her and held a modified riding crop to her lips: she knew she must kiss it, and she did. The crop had a silver-plated handle and the little loop at the striking end had been replaced by a thick, solid triangle of leather. It was a deceptively harmless-looking tool that could hurt a great deal, and she knew that it would hurt her now. He was moving away from where she could see him, and she was aware that he would soon be behind her and the beating would begin. She tried to steady her breathing, to be ready, wanting to please him and perform perfectly, but the first blow fell sooner than she expected, and she let out a little yip of shock. The hard, stiff leather sent a fiery blast of pain through her nerve endings, and several more blows landed on her arse in rapid succession. Helen sagged a little in the stocks, then straddled her legs and braced herself: if she collapsed in public the Master would be furious, and the consequences would be appalling. She tried to find the dark joy inside herself, the ecstasy of submission that he had told her was what made her truly herself.

~

Ricky was sweating and breathing hard. His hands were cuffed together and attached to a short length of chain which hung from a sturdy hook in the ceiling. He was naked and, in some tiny, unimportant part of his mind, he quite enjoyed the idea that some of the men in the room would be shocked or even outraged by this. Get a good eyeful, he thought, and that goes for the girls as well. Because of his good looks and general cockiness, plenty of people just assumed he was a top who might make a token gesture of accepting a spanking now and again: there had been girls who tried to win his favours by offering absolute submission. Ricky had played with some, now and again, but rapidly disabused them of the idea that he might want a female plaything who surrendered herself to him full-time. He'd always loved submitting in public, losing all control and yet, once it was all over, walking happily through the crowd to reclaim a seat, have a drink and resume a conversation.

Natasha and Malorie had bound his hands, then taken turns with a soft suede flogger on his back, and his arse, and even his inner thighs once they'd pulled his trousers down and slid his boots off. That flogger, which he ruefully remembered selling to Natasha last summer, started off deceptively sensuous, but the cumulative effect was something else again. Also, at some point, they had switched to using Malorie's best scarlet leather cat, its heavy tails making more of an impact, more than enough to push him through the pain/pleasure barrier.

Now Malorie was standing in front of him, tall enough in her heels to touch her forehead against his without having to stretch up. She gripped his jaw with one hand, digging her long nails lightly into his flesh, and kissed him deeply, her other hand reaching down to fondle his hot, distended cock. He felt a light, cool pressure between his arse cheeks, and realised that Natasha was applying lube to his anus. She was going to bugger him, then. Right there in the club, with Malorie's arms round him, he was going to have his arsehole plundered with Natasha's wicked red strap-on. He groaned in happy anticipation, and Malorie kissed him again.

~

Helen was crying; she couldn't help it. The Master had attached weighted clamps to her nipples, and with every third stroke of the crop on her arse he would pause, stretch the crop under her body, and strike the weights so that they swung from side to side, and the cruel little teeth of the clamps bit in deeper to her tender teats. As often happened when the Master was causing her pain, she found her memory racing back to the things he had told her in the earliest stages of her slave training, about how she would learn to accept and enjoy everything he did, and how wonderful she would feel when she understood the art of true submission. As always, the memories were muzzy but somehow even more exciting than if they had been clear: she saw his cruel face looming over her, snarling at her then abruptly softening as he told her how much she loved it. She had only had the most minimal experiences of fetish clubs or BDSM sex before she met him – indeed, she had found her first club trip and the couple of people she had met via online kinky personal ads a deep disappointment. She had been about to decide that she must have made a mistake in thinking BDSM was what she really needed when she encountered the Master on a femsub website. It had taken several weeks of emails and chat forum exchanges before she had agreed to meet him in the flesh, but now she understood that he had known what she really wanted all along. She had been drifting, it felt like, for years, and it had been no hardship to give notice on her bedsit and move in with the Master, allow him to take control of her whole life. She had nothing else to do with it.

Suddenly the harsh cropping ceased, and she choked on her sobs, listening intently to see if she was to be given any new commands. The music in here was quieter, but still made it necessary to concentrate.

'Take them off her,' the Master was saying. 'She screams so magnificently.' Unfamiliar hands fumbled at her breasts, the nipple clamps fell away, and the agony of the blood rushing back into the previously compressed flesh made her howl like a banshee. Before she had really accepted that she was screaming, she felt the Master's hard fingers penetrating her snatch, and his thumb rubbing firmly round and round her clit and, knees almost buckling entirely, she changed the pitch of her cry from pain to orgasmic satisfaction.

~

Queueing for the cloakroom at the end of the night, comfortably sated and hoping they wouldn't have to wait too long for a cab, Malorie and Ricky ran into Dizzy again. Unusually, the propmaker was looking rather put out, shoulders hunched and lips pursed. 'You all right?' Malorie couldn't help asking. Dizzy sniffed. 'Oh, I just think some people are fucking stupid, darling. I mean, really!'

'What's up?' Ricky enquired, and Dizzy gave a quick toss of the head in the direction of The Master, who was talking to a couple well-known for their organising activities, both of them being leading lights in the planning of the forthcoming Kinktastic event. 'Oh, Mr and Mrs Muppet have only invited that dickhead to give a workshop at Kinktastic. All about how REAL women submit properly, crap like that. How can anyone take him seriously when he's got the manners of a slug, and that poor little cow clearly doesn't have enough sense to come in out of the rain?'

Malorie smiled, her head on Ricky's shoulder. 'Don't let it get to you, Dizz. We can just go along and heckle. Most people will, won't they?' It was a comment she would remember in later weeks with a kind of rueful amusement.

CHAPTER THREE

Ricky wasn't used to being alone for this much time. He'd got out of the habit. Though he'd technically lived by himself for some years before meeting Malorie, there had usually been girlfriends or playmates at least half the week and, if not any of those, friends to go drinking with. Right now, he didn't feel he could deal with anyone in any more depth than the normal interactions of Thrillers. Friends might probe, however kindly, and there was nothing he could say to them. He had known it would be several days, if not longer, before he heard anything from Malorie but knowing it in advance hadn't really prepared him for how it would feel: day after day, night after night, the bed too big and too empty without her. Since they got this place and moved in together, they'd hardly ever been apart for more than a few hours at a time, and he was almost angry with himself for finding it so difficult.

On the fourth night, he dreamt of her, dreamt he had her back in the restraint chair in the playroom they'd set up in the flat's smaller bedroom. She was naked, blindfolded, her thighs spread by the chair's v-shaped seat, her ankles cuffed to the chairlegs and her wrists cuffed to its solid wooden arms. He had been tormenting her with a small, sharp-bladed knife, running the tip of it over her breasts, using it to tease her big, pink nipples erect. She'd been panting and gasping, urging him on, telling him he could do anything with her, and after a while he'd dropped the knife and forced his cock into her mouth, pulling her hair while she sucked him. He'd woken up hard and erect, almost painfully so, and got out of bed, pacing the room for nearly half an hour before he finally got one of her black leather gloves from the dressing table drawer, put it on and wanked himself off, almost sobbing her name when the spunk burst out of him. If she walked in now he'd put her up against the wall and fuck her, then bend her over the kitchen table and fuck her arse, then he'd thrash her, and then he'd kneel at her feet and taste her pussy, drown in her juices. He shook his head, telling himself to get a fucking grip, it couldn't be much longer, and stumbled back to bed.

~

The next day, he got her stuff ready, as she'd asked him to do in the run-up to her departure. The little spycams and miniature audio recorders, ordered off the Internet, had arrived the day before she left, and it didn't take Ricky too long to sew the sound recorders into various accessories; the seams of a corset, the back of an elaborate presentation collar, the waistband of a skirt. He concealed the cameras in the inner pocket of her favourite holdall, on the grounds that, if the Master actually bothered to come along with Malorie when she returned for her belongings, he might veto items of clothing on some or other dipshit grounds but was hardly likely to quibble about the choice of luggage. They hadn't been able to predict quite how this part of their plan would pan out, but they'd both agreed that it was far too risky for her to take the spyware with her on her first visit. They did not hold out much hope of the cameras being any use, anyway, and had really only bought the things because they were on special offer. Still, Ricky thought, they might get some interesting imagery in the long run. There might be a few photo opportunities, and it wouldn't do any harm to be ready for them.

'He'll let me come home to get my stuff,' Malorie had said. 'Bound to. If he doesn't let the girls go home to get their stuff then it might make it look a little bit like he's, you know, holding people against their will and all that. Serious shit. Someone's ex or mates or mum might actually call the police on his arse.'

'That's true,' Ricky had conceded. They were lying in bed, her head on his shoulder, her leg across his. He had his arm round her and, as they talked, he was sliding his hand further down, caressing her bum cheeks and slowly tracing a finger down between them. 'Mind you, not all his slave girls live with him, do they? However many he's got. You might be home the next day. You might only get a weekly appointment. He's so in demand, isn't he?'

He felt her nod against him. 'So they say. But the only one he's ever seen out with is that poor cow on a lead. Maybe the rest of them are buried in his cellar or something. We still don't really know what happened to Indianna to freak her out like that, do we?'

Ricky flinched a little; he couldn't help it. Indianna had been with The Master for a while and then, apparently, had left him, or been dumped by him: she was alive and well but the word was that she wanted nothing further to do with the fetish scene, and it had been preying on Malorie's mind. Ricky wondered, again, about the wisdom of the plan. So much of it was so vague, so dependent on luck and other random factors.

'No way. Shit! Malorie, if you think there's anything like that going on, you get the hell out of there. I mean it, run like fuck.' He got both arms round her, held her tightly. 'I mean it,' he said again.

Malorie kissed him. 'Don't worry, love. I'll run if I have to. And I'll be home as quick as I can, whatever. But it just might take a few days, that's all.'

~

During the summer, Malorie and Ricky had seen the Master several more times, and Malorie had noticed quite a lot of online discussion about him and his alleged Method in the run up to Kinktastic. The Master himself occasionally participated in these squabbles, usually posting with vicious condescension but never appearing to become truly angry with his critics. Apparently, he held very select parties from time to time, strictly heterosexual, strictly dominant men and submissive women. 'Well, that rules us out,' Ricky had said, when this came up in conversation at the main monthly market for fetish and adult goods. 'Funny how some people are so scared of switches. Mind you, we wouldn't want to bloody go, would we?'

'Well, we haven't been invited,' said Harry Nicholas, the source of this piece of gossip. He gave his wife Cath a light slap on the rump, and she laughed. 'We don't want to go, either,' she said. 'Though I wouldn't mind seeing his place, apparently it's out of this world.'

Malorie and Ricky had heard this before, but they were still none the wiser about what the Master actually did with his life. Cath and Harry thought they'd noticed some rumour that The Master was going to write a book setting out his Female Training Method. 'What's he going to call it? Mein Kampf?'

sniggered Malorie, and one or two people nearby looked mildly outraged.

'Whenever anyone does anything really radical, some people are always jealous.' said a short, chunky woman wearing rather too much jewellery. Her name was Angela Curver, and she usually had a lot to say for herself: about the joy of submission and the importance of not being afraid of your own desires, and the rest. Few people had ever seen her actually bend over in public, though. Malorie snorted derisively, but Ricky laid a hand on her arm: no point in starting a ruck, the woman could easily claim she'd not been talking to them at all. Anyway, The Master wasn't that big a deal, he would probably be flavour-of-the-summer then either vanish, as so many of the gobbiest did after a season or two, or settle down into a more relaxed give-and-take with other kinks, like the rest tended to. It wasn't till after Kinktastic that Malorie and Ricky really started to think that something ought to be done.

~

Malorie didn't get back to Thrillers until the Friday, a whole week after she'd knocked on the Master's door and offered to serve him. For the first couple of days, she had wondered, almost obsessively, when and how she could ask to collect her belongings, or leave with a promise to return. He seemed to have simply decided that she should stay; he exhibited no curiousity about the rest of her life, and Malorie thought this a little strange, but wasn't sure how to address it. The Master had treated her with a cold contempt, barely addressing a word to her and speaking mainly to Helen when he wanted Malorie to do something. For Malorie, who had been used to the constantly-busy life of any small business person, life in the Master's house was actually quite boring, or it would have been if she could summon up the energy to be bored. There was another woman in the household, whose name Malorie was not told, and who never seemed to speak beyond the absolute basics of 'Yes sir, no sir'; who wore a maid's uniform and did the bulk of the housework, but Malorie was obliged to perform certain basic household tasks: washing up, some cleaning, nothing too demanding – except that at least twice a day, the Master would seize her, drag her to the dungeon and beat her. Yet there were also long hours when she was ordered into the little annexe room where she and Helen slept, and just left there. She found she slept a lot, and in some part of her mind she wondered if she ought to worry about this.

She didn't know what had become of her raincoat: though Helen was sometimes dressed in fetish costumes or lingerie, Malorie was never told or expected to wear anything apart from her ankleboots. The beatings were always painful, though none quite as harsh as the first night, but

Malorie found it almost impossible to ride the pain, transform it into excitement. Ricky had sometimes whipped her harder, but when Ricky did it, even during the cruellest roleplay, arousal would course through her veins, and by the end of it she'd be dripping wet and begging him to fuck her. She began to wonder if the Master would fuck her: if he ever fucked, even. Nothing he did or said suggested in any way that he lusted after her, apart from that look in his eyes when he'd first opened the door. To Helen he was charming, if a little condescending, but quite often affectionate, and Helen seemed to be blossoming on a daily basis. She was spending a lot of time with The Master while Malorie remained in the annexe room, but if Malorie made even a tentative enquiry as to what she was doing, Helen would only say that it was 'part of her training.' After the first night, she had made no more sexual overtures to Malorie even though the two of them were still sleeping in the same bed. Always, when Malorie was being beaten in the evening, Helen would be either ordered, or permitted – Malorie was unsure – to kneel beside the whipping stool and watch. Both girls would then be ordered to bed, after the Master had gone through the evening ritual of drinking a glass of brandy and giving one to each of the girls. He would ring a bell to order this brandy, and the maid would bring it in on a tray. On the second night she did this, Malorie almost dared to speak to her, but when she raised her eyes to the maid's face, something in the woman's look of smug contempt chilled her, and made her drop her gaze and back away.

She supposed the brandy was what made her sleep so heavily at night, even after the amount she was sleeping during the day: she felt groggy and strange in the mornings, with little or no appetite, and an odd conviction that she was missing something important. Thoughts seemed to intrude into her brain, thoughts that made little or no sense. She tried to think of Ricky, even though it made her feel homesick but, somehow, he seemed so very far away.

On the fourth night, the Master ordered both the girls to the dungeon as usual but, instead of cuffing Malorie to the whipping block, he instructed her to kneel, and turned to Helen.

'Don't think I haven't noticed,' he said. 'Get into position, cunt.' Helen, biting her lip, bent over the block and spread her legs, balancing herself. She wrapped her hands round the sturdy wooden legs and held on; the Master didn't bother to cuff her. Malorie wondered what fault or sin the Master was implying Helen had committed: she couldn't say she had noticed any lapse in behaviour. Feeling dazed and distant, she watched the Master select a thick rubber paddle with three circular holes in the middle, and stand behind Helen, lightly tapping her arse with the thing.

Then he drew it back and laid on the first hard blow. Helen grunted but didn't move, and the Master struck again, then again. Helen groaned, then as the steady, brutal blows continued, began to let out short cries of pain. The Master, shirtless and attired only in thick leather trousers and heavy boots, beat her steadily for several minutes, until she was crying piteously and his bald head and muscular torso were gleaming with sweat.

He turned to Malorie and held out the paddle.

'Put this away, cunt, and bring the lubricant from the cupboard next to the implement rack.' Quickly, if a little clumsily, Malorie got to her feet and did as she was told. The Master had unzipped his trousers and was stroking his cock, a sight which simultaneously made Malorie's skin crawl and somewhere deep down, she realised with a sense of hot shame, aroused her. He took the bottle of lube from her and anointed himself, then turned back to the still-sobbing Helen and pulled her arse cheeks apart. Malorie expected him simply to thrust cruelly into the other girl's abused bottom, but the Master took his time penetrating Helen and, once he had achieved full access, fucked her languorously, teasingly, almost gently. After a while, he sank into her as far as he could go, his body tensed for a moment and he gave a deep, harsh sigh, then withdrew and stepped back. Helen hadn't stopped crying yet, and didn't do so when the Master said, 'You're still not where you ought to be, cunt. Finish yourself. Now. On the floor.'

She lifted herself off the whipping block then crouched, in obvious pain, yet as she began to finger her pussy, her sobs quietened and then turned into lust-filled moans, before she slumped back against the wall and shuddered in orgasm. Malorie, watching, felt her own sex fill with heat; she wasn't happy to feel turned on by anything the Master did, but her juices were definitely starting to flow. She tensed her quim muscles and set her teeth.

The Master rang the bell for the maid to bring in the brandy, but when it had been drunk, he took hold of a handful of Helen's hair and lifted her to her feet.

'Go to my room and wait.,' he told her and Helen, her face transformed by something like religious ecstasy, clattered away unsteadily on her heels. Malorie remained on her knees, not daring to move. Was he going to beat her and fuck her now? Was he going to make her suck him off? If so, could she handle doing it? Malorie loved to suck cock, but the idea of sucking this man's cock terrified her. The Master turned to his rack of toys and selected a pair of handcuffs.

'Stand,' he ordered and, when she obeyed, he cuffed her hands behind her back.

'Now go to bed,' he said, and left the dungeon without even looking to see if she would do as instructed. Bewildered, uneasy and uncomfortable,

Malorie went through to the sleeping area and somehow managed to get herself onto the bed though, with her hands cuffed as they were, she couldn't do anything about either removing her boots or drawing up the blanket. She closed her eyes, but was utterly tormented by a nagging, maddening itch of frustration in her quim. The only thing that eased it, in the end, was squeezing her thighs together hard and thinking desperately of Ricky.

~

It was a cold, bright autumn Friday, with the wind blowing swirls of leaves all over the place: though Thrillers was in a busy suburban high street, there were trees planted at intervals up and down the pavement, and all of them – a mix of rowans and beeches – had shed their foliage, and the bulk of it seemed to want to scuttle under the door and into the shop. Ricky had spent half the morning wielding a broom at intervals before deciding to give up and just do it at the end of the day. He was brooding over an unread spanking magazine when the doorbell jangled, and the Master walked in with Malorie behind him.

'She's come for her things,' the Master said in a tone of such condescension that Ricky couldn't stop his fists clenching. He took a deep breath in, let it out and said, 'OK.' Everything was rushing into his head at once: he'd prepared things but not actually packed her a bag, should he go upstairs and fetch it all for her, throw her stuff at her in an outraged-dumped role? They had, really, expected her to be allowed to return home by herself, and Ricky felt a moment's deep relief that he had distributed the gadgetry amongst both clothing and luggage, no matter what happened now she would get some of it back into Shithead's house with her. Almost immediately, though, he had a sudden lurch of what he tried to tell himself was irrational panic: after this long, was she coming back for the spyware? Or had the Master taken her over?

He looked at her, standing two clear paces behind the bald bastard: she wore the same raincoat she'd left in, the same boots, but her ankles were linked with short-chain silver handcuffs and her hands, behind her back, might be cuffed as well. She had her head bowed, so he had no way of making eye contact or making any kind of guess as to what she was thinking.

The door opened again with a cheery dingaling of the bell, and Ricky looked towards it. The Master rather ostentatiously didn't notice, and Malorie remained in her submissive stance.

The girl who walked in was someone Ricky could never remember the name of: petite and pretty with bright pink hair, she generally seemed to know what was going on without ever participating in much of it. She smiled as she walked in, then headed immediately for a rail of PVC skirts and bustiers and began to flick through it.

'OK,' Ricky said again, cautiously. 'Malorie, you want to go upstairs, do you?' He thought he sounded stupid, but at the same time he was throwing her some sort of a cue. Malorie didn't move, but the Master grinned. 'You can take her upstairs. She'll need your help to pack. I'll make sure no one steals anything valuable.'

Ricky got that one all right. I've stolen your girlfriend and I'm rubbing your nose in it. But it did mean a minute or two alone with her, which was what he'd hoped for.

She moved towards him as though she was sleepwalking, taking little short steps so that the chain between her ankles jingled, never once lifting her head. Miss Pink Hair looked up once and smiled in a cheerfully conspiratorial, complicit way, then returned her attention to a black tutu-style skirt with a laced waistband.

~

Malorie had been beginning to worry about getting back to the shop to get the recording equipment. It nagged at her at intervals, yet it was hard to keep track of the days, and of what she was doing, when her thoughts were more and more obsessed with whether or when the Master was going to fuck her. She wanted it and didn't want it, and she wanted to get the spyware and finish things, and at the same time, there was no rush, was there? Then, that Friday morning, the Master had looked at her over the breakfast table and said, 'Malorie, today you're going to get whatever little things you want from your old home. I would like to see you attractively dressed, and I know you have some appropriate clothing.'

Knowing by now what was expected of her, Malorie bowed her head and murmured, 'Thank you, Master.'

'Finish your meal,' the Master said, and went on with his own. Shortly afterwards, he had sent Helen to the sleeping annex and told her to stay there. Coming back up to the kitchen, where Malorie was waiting, he had produced the linked ankle cuffs and put her in them, then her own PVC raincoat, and ordered her to put it on. After that, he had cuffed her hands behind her back and marched her out of the house with a hand on the back of her neck

His car was a plain black BMW with tinted windows: he ordered her into the passenger seat and instructed her to remain silent for the drive back into town and to the shop. It was difficult to get into the car with both wrists and ankles cuffed, and she had to bite her lip not to object to the impracticality of it as he stood there watching her, smirking at her struggles. Once she was seated, he bent over her and fastened the seatbelt, before pushing her head to one side and placing a swift but telling lovebite on her throat.

He drove aggressively but reasonably well, and it didn't take very long to get to Thrillers. Malorie had a little flash of amusement when she was obliged to get out of the car and scuttle up to the doorway in her ankle cuffs, naked under the raincoat: it was not at all the first time anyone had turned up in full fetish mode and role, it just hadn't been her before. During the journey, she had felt her head clearing, away from the stifling house, yet she remained as still and silent as she had been ordered to be.

~

Once inside, she felt a profound wish to run to Ricky, and throw herself into his arms, but did her best to control it. They couldn't have rehearsed this bit beforehand, they were both having to play it by ear: would he respond to an order from the Master to fetch things for her? That would be OK, but perhaps the Master would insist on accompanying her to her bedroom and watching her pack. He wouldn't suspect anything, of course, but how would Ricky deal with that? How should Ricky deal with it? Malorie was alarmed to realise that she wasn't at all sure what she wanted to happen at this point.

When he gave the command for her to go upstairs with Ricky, she was almost shocked – why would the creep make it that easy for them? Then she understood that the Master was gloating. He was enjoying the possibility of humiliating Ricky further, utterly convinced that Malorie belonged to him now. He couldn't have a clue that he was giving Malorie and her lover an advantage. They would have a few minutes together, if nothing else.

Ricky wasn't really looking at her, he just turned away and made for the stairs, muttering, 'Come on, then,' over his shoulder. Malorie glanced back at the Master, but he, too, had turned his attention from her, and was gazing intently at the pretty girl browsing among the clothes. Malorie felt a sharp pang of annoyance, then anxiety: what was the matter with her? Neither she nor Ricky spoke until they had gone up the stairs and Ricky had unlocked the door that led from the shop to their flat. Then he said, still not looking at her, 'Your stuff's ready. Still want it all, do you?'

'Ricky - ' she said, desperately, suddenly sure she was going to cry and frantic not to. She stumbled through the door after him, kicking it so that it shut, and then Ricky turned round to her and held out his arms. She stumbled against him, unable to hold him because of her cuffed hands, and he grabbed her chin and lifted it to give her one long, hard kiss. 'You all right?' he said when it was done. 'Is he - ' He clearly couldn't finish, but now Malorie felt her strength come back. 'It's fine. He's a wanker but it's fine.' Just the touch of Ricky's mouth on hers had re-empowered her, her senses clearing, as though a surrounding mist was thinning and drifting away. 'Look, it's hypnosis, most of it. I think that's how he's doing it. Subliminals. And definitely drugs. too. Is it all sorted?' She waved towards the bag on the bed and Ricky nodded. 'Collar, corset. Some stuff in the inside pocket. OK, come on, let's get your clothes together. Tell me what you want and then we'll go back down. Do you think it'll take much longer?'

She shook her head. 'Nah. A day or two, maybe. I promise.'

It didn't take long to throw a selection of her least-valuable fetish outfits into the bag, along with a plain black tracksuit: she wanted to add a pair of trainers but decided it might be unwise to do so. Getting back down the stairs was trickier than ascending had been; she felt slightly dizzy and once or twice caught her heel on the step; Ricky took hold of her arm and guided her, and she struggled not to lean into him or kiss his face or neck.

~

In the shop, the Master was examining a rack of expensive leather floggers and stroking his little beard. He must have heard Malorie's heels clattering on the wooden floor, but he left it a full minute before turning his attention to her.

'Ready?' he asked, and she nodded. He ignored Ricky entirely, and marched out of the shop, not even bothering to hold the door open for Malorie, who had almost to scuttle in her hobbled footwear to catch up with him and get through the door before it shut. Ricky couldn't bear to watch them drive away, so he simply stood behind the counter, trying to steady his breathing.

'Oh, Lord, Ricky, I'm so sorry!' It was the pink-haired girl, who Ricky had pretty much forgotten about. 'There was something about it in the SM Link chatroom, about her leaving you for the Master. It must be awful for you.'

Ricky looked down into her eager little face, avid for gossip, and wanted to punish her. Well, he wanted to punish someone, anyway. So, they were talking about it on SM Link, were they? Wonder who'd started that rumour.

'I could be consoled,' he said, menacingly, and the girl giggled and bit her lip. 'I suppose it was a bit naughty of me to say anything,' she offered, lowering her eyes. 'But quite a few of the girls would be happy to, you know. Console you. Is that out of order too?'

'Just a bit, isn't it?' Ricky came out from behind the counter and went to the shop door, where he turned the sign round to read Closed. 'It's all a bit out of order, right now.'

CHAPTER FOUR

The Kinktastic event had been the talk of the scene for months before it actually took place. For the first time in years there was going to be a full-on, one-day festival of sexual diversity, sexual politics, education and entertainment. Well, that was the idea, Ricky and Malorie had agreed, but the reality was quite probably going to be a load of stalls, a few workshops run by egomaniacs or well-meaning idiots, and hopefully a reasonably good club night to end up with.. They had secured the services of Madame Natasha's occasional maid Esmeralda (or Les, as he was known when not en femme), who had been on the scene for 10 years and had a rather cynical view of big events, to run the shop on the day so both of them could attend the whole thing. The Master had been posting quite a bit on various discussions about his Method, about the natural rightness of female submission to male authority, and had been getting, rather to Malorie's annoyance, pretty much equal amounts of support and condemnation. She had, she would admit to anyone who asked, been supplying a fair bit of the latter, and it hadn't involved her usual tease-the-dom-to-get-a-seeing-to fun and games. She had said to Ricky, more than once that there, was something seriously off-key about The Master. Ricky, who also thought the man was a creep, was less bothered about it, but he did agree that there was no good reason for The Master to have been asked to run any kind of workshops at Kinktastic.

'We could have run one for them if they were desperate, couldn't we?' he mentioned a few days before the event, when Malorie had come down into the shop spitting with rage after another online battle with Angela Curver about where you should draw the line. Malorie had opined that people who made such a big noise about forced play, even if they were allegedly just living out a deep lifestyle fantasy, shouldn't be made mini-celebs of as it sent out the wrong message, Angela reckoning that Malorie was being judgemental and had the wrong idea about people who didn't switch.

'What, How to Open A Shop?' Malorie asked, mildly intrigued. 'Or How to Switch?'

'How to Start Fights Online, I thought,' Ricky said, and when she grabbed one of the newest soft silicon buttplugs off the shelf and chased him behind the counter with it, things could have got a little entertaining if a couple of customers had not chosen that moment to walk in through the door.

But it was true that the Master was an unusual, and not entirely popular, addition to the list of workshop co-ordinators and guest speakers.

~

Kinktastic took place at the end of September, in a community arts venue with a longstanding open-minded attitude, and Malorie and Ricky spent the first couple of hours catching up with assorted old friends and exploring the range of goods sold to see if there were any new traders around who might be amenable to supplying stock for Thrillers. One of the main topics of conversation on the day, they found, was that The Master was doing not one but two talks, something which, it seemed, no one outside of the organising committee had known about till they arrived and read the schedule of events. The first of these Happenings, as Malorie referred to them, was for men only, and involved an admission charge which did include a password to access the Master's Domination Method website, the second was open to 'All Females but Only Females.'

'That's the one that's going to be heckler central, isn't it?' Ricky had remarked, loud enough to draw giggles from a couple of bystanders and a look of disdain from Angela Curver.

'Not at all,' a voice had said close behind him, and both Ricky and Malorie had turned to see The Master, flanked by a couple of musclebound, leather-clad men they had never met before. 'In the presence of a Master, all women must obey their truest instincts.' He had looked Malorie up and down slowly, then licked his lips and moved away, leaving an annoyingly appreciative silence in his wake. The two henchmen, or bodyguards, or whatever they were, moved off with him, and Malorie put a hand on the back of Ricky's neck to draw him close. 'I think that arsehole is actually challenging me,' she had purred. 'We're not bloody paying for you to go to his boys' own wankfest, but I'm definitely going to check out the girls' one.'

Ricky had merely nodded at the time, though both of them had previously envisaged checking out the Master's talk together, thinking it would be good for a laugh if nothing else. Ricky didn't think much of the Master, but then he didn't care for pomposity in any shape or form: he didn't have Malorie's growing anger at the Master's publicized insistence that all women were really pure submissives who just needed to be trained but, Ricky supposed, that was because he wasn't a woman. He would wonder, later, what would have happened if he'd talked Malorie out of going to the workshop.

~

The Master's True Female Submission Lesson, as it was billed, took place in one of the upstairs rooms, and someone had clearly spent a fair bit of time changing its ambience from ordinary, institutional space to something more appropriate. Black fabric had been hung at the windows, blocking out all natural light, more black fabric draped over one large table at the front, and the chairs were set in semicircular rows, facing it. On the table were two large, ball-shaped lamps, which were lit, and an incense burner, flanked by a leather flogger and two heavy canes. To the left of the door was another table with a tray of filled cups and a punchbowl containing a dark red liquid. The Master's two companions, who Malorie guessed might have been the ones doing all the fabric-draping and chair-moving, sat at either side of the top table while the Master himself stood by the punchbowl. 'Now don't be afraid,' he was saying. 'You have nothing to fear from greater self-knowledge. Please relax, have a drink if you would like one, take a seat.'

His eyes lingered on Malorie a moment, but she noticed that he gave the same assessing stare to some of the other women and told herself not to see anything personal in it. She took one of the cups from the table and sniffed the contents before taking a sip: not all the women were accepting the offer of a drink and it occurred to her that they thought it might be drugged. She managed not to giggle: as if the mad bastard would try to dope a whole roomful of women in the middle of a bloody great public event like this. 'What's in it?' another girl asked, and the Master's smile grew wide and innocent. 'Passionfruit, pomegranate, grape juice and a little brandy. I find it stimulates the senses in a suitable way. Perhaps I should have said, it does contain alcohol so if you don't drink, then perhaps it's not for you.'

Malorie sipped her drink again: she couldn't detect the brandy, so the tight git probably hadn't put more than a single measure in the whole bowlful. Natasha Williams, who shot Malorie a mischievous wink when the Master wasn't looking, had already drained one cup and sneaked another before sitting down. Malorie was tempted to go and sit beside her: of the other women she recognised, there was no one she particularly liked, but she supposed it would be bad form to sit with Madame Natasha. The two of them might not be able to resist the temptation to take the piss, and she did want to hear what the Master had to say before tearing into it.

The room was now two-thirds full, but it didn't seem as though anyone else was likely to show up, so one of the leathermen got up, walked to the door and shut it firmly, while the other did something to the lights so they dimmed down. The Master walked up to the table and leaned nonchalantly against it.

'You may find the trappings theatrical,' he observed with a rueful smile. 'But then, what's wrong with a little theatre when we are finding our way to our truest selves?'

The lights, while low, seemed to pulse slightly as he talked on, and Malorie began to feel rather bored. He was talking a lot of dull but basically harmless guff about honesty and self-knowledge and knowing what you wanted: she began to wonder if she and a few others weren't making a monster out of someone who was really just a hardcore scene player with a good pose going on. It was a pretty stylish sort of schtick really: not that much malice in it that she could detect. After a while, though, he did begin to say some mildly unpleasant things about the naturalness of female submission, and the arrogance of women who refused to accept male dominance, but it was somehow quite hard to single out any particularly outrageous statement, and her thoughts kept wandering away. She found herself focusing on his hands, which moved in graceful gestures: they were strong hands, powerful hands... She was beginning to feel almost sleepy, losing track of time, and then quite suddenly he picked up one of the canes and swished it through the air.

'In pain is where you find relief, in servitude is where you find freedom. My lessons may be harsh, but they are necessary. And when I deem a female worthy of serving Me and call her to my service, then she will only resist if she is lying to herself and content to live dishonestly. If she is willing to accept her true self, then she will come when I decide to call her, night or day, no matter what. But the journey to acceptance is a long one.'

He almost bowed, but it wasn't quite a bow, and then the lights came right up to maximum brightness, really suddenly, and Malorie found herself joining the other women in a huge burst of applause. She looked down at her hands as she smacked them together, and suddenly shuddered.

~

It was the day after Malorie had been taken back to Thrillers to collect her clothes, and the Master was entertaining guests tonight. Midway through the afternoon, when both Helen and Malorie had been engaged in dusting the upper rooms, the Master had come upon them and said, 'It's time to find out how well your training is progressing, cunts. Go and make yourselves fit to be displayed.'

Malorie had been a little confused but Helen had seemed pleased and excited.

'There's going to be a party, so we need to look really good, come on, you can have first shower.'

One thing Malorie could never complain of in the Master's house was a lack of bathroom facilities: though the dungeon annexe where she and Helen slept was dark, basic and prison-like, the rest of the house was reasonably normal, if a little Gothic in its décor. Much of the topmost floor consisted of bedrooms, at least half of them with ensuites: there were two rooms which Malorie had not been allowed into. She presumed, she told herself, that one of them contained a coffin for the Master to relax in at night. Even the ground floor, apart from the two rooms dedicated to BDSM behaviour, was entirely everyday in terms of fixtures and fittings. When you came out of the dungeon, the door on the other side of the hallway led down a corridor to a comfortably appointed wet room with shower and toilet. Next to this room was a smaller room with fitted wardrobes, where Malorie had been instructed to place her belongings when the Master brought her back to his house. Of the three wardrobes, two had been empty and the third contained only a limited amount of clothing, mainly fetish wear but a few odds and ends of streetclothes which were obviously Helen's: Malorie had initially wondered if this meant there had previously been more slavegirls living in the house, or if the Master was simply ready to enslave more. Having showered, she went there to select something to wear for the party. It occurred to her that this room was probably the least likely to contain any hidden cameras under the Master's control: she had glimpsed telltale red lights in both the play rooms and the large sitting room on the first floor. He was unlikely to bother about filming them dressing; clothing didn't appear to be one of his fetishes, and now she contemplated digging out one of her own spycams. While she was trying to work out how to conceal one of the wretched things somewhere on her person, though, Helen came into the dressing room and the opportunity vanished. Malorie silently thanked Ricky for his brilliance in hiding the sound recorders in her clothes before she collected them, and picked up her presentation collar. She had never liked it very much. It made her keep her chin up and her neck unnaturally straight, and was singularly uncomfortable: at home, they had only ever really used it for photoshoots. Tonight, though, she was glad of the discomfort, it seemed to clear her head and give her some strength of purpose. She was aware, as she had briefly told Ricky, that the Master was giving both her and probably Helen some kind of tranquilising drugs, probably administered in the nightly glass of brandy, but she didn't think the drug was all that powerful: she felt groggy and her thought processes were sometimes slower, but it didn't take much to revive her sense of self. Once she'd put the collar on, she ran her fingers carefully along the bottom edge until she felt a tiny lump which hadn't been there before: this would be the recorder. Malorie was not very gadget-minded, so she had only listened to the essential parts of Ricky's explanation the night before she left: that she should squeeze the thing firmly to set it working, that it would record for about 24 hours, and that she should either bring it home with her or find some way of getting it back to him: the device needed to be plugged into some kind of mothership to be played back. She gave it a sharp squeeze and hoped it would work or, if this one didn't work, one of the others would. Fancy gadgets bought from funny websites had a wearying tendency to be completely useless when push came to shove.

'Ooh, you look amazing,' Helen cooed. 'What's that like to wear? I'd love one of those,'

In answering the other girl's chatter and praising her appearance in turn, Malorie felt her confidence returning. She'd get something on the bastard tonight, and then she could go home.

~

Kneeling on the floor beside the sofa, holding a small silver tray with bowls of nuts and crisps, Malorie felt her cheeks burn with humiliation as she recognised the voice of Angela Curver. There were quite a lot of people at the party, and several of them knew her: as yet, no one had tried to engage her in conversation, all abiding by the protocols of lifestyle dominance and submission which meant that a slave was not to be treated as an ordinary person without the slave's master or mistress' permission for this to happen. Angela was indeed airing her views about protocol right now, and Malorie ventured a careful glance upwards to see what the other woman was doing. She had to admit, she thought, that Angela looked good: a plain leather collar and cuffs were all she wore above the waist, and she had on a flared leather miniskirt that flattered her chunky legs. It was difficult to judge who she was with, though Malorie knew she would be accompanied by a man who was, technically at least, her master for the evening: though the rules of the party had not been spelled out to her it was obvious that it was a night for male dominants and their female slaves, no singles permitted. Otherwise, it was just like any of the many BDSM house parties Malorie had attended previously, conversations a random blend of mundane topics, kinky techniques and their application, and fetish scene gossip. Now and then, some of the last category would include mentions of herself and the fact that she had left Ricky for the Master: this hurt and maddened Malorie far more than she had anticipated it would. She kept hoping that the Master would be unable to resist the temptation to brag about his Method, but every time anyone asked a question within Malorie's hearing, the Master simply brushed it off.

She began to feel wretchedly miserable, and wondered if she was wasting her time on a ridiculous mission that might end up making her a laughing stock. The Master himself was ostentatiously ignoring her, and though a certain amount of tying up and erotic torturing was going on in all corners of the big sitting room – with probably more in the dungeon – none of it was in her line of sight and it was becoming obvious that none of it tonight was going to involve her participation. It took a great deal of self-control to continue kneeling, holding her tray, when Angela Curver, addressing a predominantly male group of relative newbies, embarked on a monologue about switches and how they always ended up embracing one role or another, and that no switch relationship could last long.

The bitch actually came over to Malorie and scooped up some nibbles from the tray she held, while declaiming in a rather pointed manner that it was obvious which one of any alleged switch couple was the dom, and which the sub, and that if the dom was inadequate, the sub would be available to any other genuine dominant who cared to take an interest.

'Cunts want to be owned, you're right.' the Master said, and Malorie managed not to start enough to spill the contents of her tray: she hadn't realised he was nearby. There was a sudden hush in the room, and Malorie heard the Master snap his fingers.

'Helen,' he said. 'Come here'. Helen had been required to walk around the room with a tray of drinks, replenishing people's glasses when necessary: now she set the tray down on a table and walked over to where the Master stood. Malorie felt that it was safe enough to raise her head and watch the proceedings, though she didn't quite dare to put down the tray she held.

Helen was wearing a bra and panties that were really just a collection of fine black leather bands which framed rather than concealed her breasts and her sex, and a heavy silver chain padlocked around her neck. She stood in front of the Master, with her hands clasped behind her back, as he reached out and grasped a handful of her dark hair.

'I own her entirely,' he said, in a pleasant, conversational tone.' Don't I, cunt?'

'Yes, Master,' Helen gasped.

'You had to work to belong to me, though, didn't you? You had to serve and prove your worth,' the Master snarled, though his words seemed to Malorie to be less addressed to Helen than to the other guests. The Master let go of Helen's hair and wiped his hands down his leather trousers. Despite the warmth of the house, he wore a full-length leather coat with a high collar and long sleeves: his bare chest glistened with sweat.

'They all want it,' he said, and now he was deliberately addressing the crowd. 'But only some of them admit it, and not all of them are worth having. This cunt Helen is mine entirely now.' He stepped back and spread his arms wide. 'I control everything about her, every minute of her day, every thought that passes through her feeble little mind. I don't even have to touch her to make her come.'

Helen was trembling and biting her lips. Malorie dared to put her tray of snacks down on the floor; no one was paying her any attention right now.

'Come,' the Master said in a tone of near-indifference, and Helen's hips jerked. She shuddered all over and gave a succession of gasping little moans.

'Feel her,' said the Master, beckoning to Angela. 'Feel how wet the cunt is. Kneel and lick it.'

Malorie held her breath, fighting a sudden desire to snort with laughter: Angela had more than once proclaimed her own heterosexuality and, as far as Malorie could tell, was not at all excited by the idea of licking another woman's pussy. However, she had publicly declared her admiration for the Master and her own submissiveness so many times that to disobey a command would make her look like an idiot. She knelt at Helen's feet and raised her lips to the other girl's pussy.

~

Malorie found her thoughts drifting back to the man's performance at Kinktastic. She had stumbled out afterwards, vaguely aware that most, if not all, of the other women looked a bit confused but, like them, she had given herself a bit of a shake and moved to go on with her day. Ricky had been in the bar when she went back downstairs, engaged in an amiable but interminable conversation about which female sci-fi characters were submissive and which were dominant. He'd seen her and held out a friendly arm, and she'd found herself almost running the last few steps to get next to him, be pulled in close to him and put her head on his shoulder. He'd put his other arm round her and the feel of his body against hers had grounded her but, when the daytime events were winding down and people were discussing who was and was not going on to the evening Kink Ball, Malorie had suddenly felt unable to face it.

'Ricky, I need to go home,' she'd hissed into his ear as they stood in the lobby, and he'd complied straight away.

Thrillers was deserted when they arrived, Les having obeyed the instructions to close up, drop the keys through the letterbox and go home at the end of the day. They walked through the closed and darkened shop to reach the flat above it, but before they even reached the counter, Malorie had fallen on her knees.

'Let me suck you,' she said. 'Let me suck you till you come in my mouth, then beat me, then fuck me.'

Ricky unzipped his leather jeans and freed his cock. This street was deserted when the shops shut, so there was unlikely to be anyone passing by and peeping through the window, and the feel of her lips sliding up and down his shaft was delicious enough anyway. He grabbed hold of her tangled silvery hair as her mouth closed round his cock, pulling her hair gently, then less gently as she sucked. She wanted rough stuff tonight, he'd give it to her. He wasn't going to come just yet; he was going to make her work for it. He fucked her mouth for a little while, then pulled out of her, one hand still tangled in her hair, and lifted her roughly to her feet. He refastened his clothes, and breathed in, looking her up and down with a knowing, teasing, malice.

'You want it nasty, do you? Get upstairs,' he breathed and, when she made for the stairs, he followed hard behind her. She made for the playroom, gasping and muttering something incoherent to herself, Ricky caught up with her, grabbed her arm and all but threw her over the whipping bench.

'Ricky, make me cry,' she whispered, and he stood stock still for a moment, feeling his cock get even harder, a tension in his chest as his fists clenched momentarily. He'd planned to start with a flogger or maybe a hand spanking, but now he turned to the rack of punishment toys and selected a heavy leather tawse that they rarely used on each other.

She was still dressed in the skimpy little black number she'd been wearing all day; in deference to Kinktastic being a daytime event, she had on a black thong and hold-up fishnets as well. He yanked the skirt up to her waist and ripped the thong right off her. He drew back and hit her once with the tawse; she shrieked. A stripe bloomed across her bottom and he hit her again, then laid on a third, even harder stroke and she burst into tears. He hit her twice more, hard as he could, and she screamed and wept, but through her sobs she was crying out, 'Yes, love, yes!'

His prick was hard, hard and throbbing, and he grabbed her by the hair again, lifting her up and hustling her out of the dungeon and into the bedroom, where he threw her onto the bed, undoing his trousers with his free hand, taking hold of his cock to shove it inside her as she opened her legs wide for him, fucking her dripping wet quim with hard possessive thrusts. Still sobbing, she clung to him, rising up underneath him, grinding herself against him, and he forced his arms underneath her writhing body, holding her tight to him, and she was clinging to him, kissing him, and they were both coming, both crying out and clutching each other, and then it was over.

'I love you,' she said shakily. 'I love you for everything. I love you because you're you.' Ricky rolled off her and pulled her back into his arms. 'You're my whole bloody world, aren't you? I love you, Malorie Jackson. Now what the fuck did that slaphead do to you?'

Malorie clung on to him; he could feel her shuddering. 'He's scum. Oh shit, I'm being stupid about this. But he's really not right. There's really something not right about him. Really, love.'

CHAPTER FIVE

It was the morning after The Master's party, and Helen and Malorie, supervised by the maid whose name Malorie had still not learned, were clearing up. Malorie had been sent peremptorily to bed some time around 3am, as the party was dying down. Helen had not been sent with her, and had not been there when a braying alarm bell woke her at 9, an hour later than usual. She had gone to the kitchen to find no one but the maid, who had served her breakfast without conversation, then told her to go and begin on the clearup of the main room.

'Should I go and get dressed first?' Malorie had asked, diffidently. The Master had, after all, told her when they went to fetch her belongings from Thrillers that he would expect to see her 'attractively dressed' in future: right now she was still, as she had been almost all the time, naked apart from her shoes, having taken off everything before going to sleep. Whether or not the Master would have cared if she slept in that damned collar or not, she certainly wasn't going to do so voluntarily, and right now she really wanted a shower, but wasn't going to risk pushing for one. The maid had shrugged, then said, 'No. Housework first.'

Helen, equally naked, had appeared just as Malorie was stacking a second load of glasses on a tray. The brunette looked tired, and there were plenty of welts, scratches and other marks of pain on her arse and her breasts, but she didn't seem particularly unhappy. Apart from a murmured morning greeting, Helen simply set to work with no further conversational overtures, and as the maid never said much as far as Malorie could tell, all three of them just got on with it in silence.

Voices drifted in from the direction of the kitchen after a while, and Malorie realised that some of the party guests must have stayed over: well, she had wondered about those guest rooms before, and this was obviously their purpose. No one came in until they had restored the room to an almost pristine state, though, and then it was only the Master who appeared, clad in a black satin robe.

'Good,' he said, and Malorie thought he sounded genuinely pleased. 'But we still have guests. Go and dress yourselves appropriately. Now.'

'Appropriately – what does he want us to wear?' Malorie hissed to Helen as they were hurrying down to the room where their clothes were kept. Helen waved her hands vaguely. 'Oh, something fetishy. Not whatever you wore last night, though. Have you got more stuff with you? Or do you want to see if any of mine fits?'

Malorie said she had plenty, thanks, because it occurred to her that, while little had been said last night about the Master's actual methods, when people were relaxing today he might let something slip, so Malorie was determined to give herself another chance at capturing an indiscretion of some sort on one of the recorders. While Helen was fannying about with different bustiers and knickers, Malorie picked through her own clothes, trying to remember which things Ricky had hidden the recording devices in. Ah, her red corset: she retrieved it, found the recorder and gave it the prescribed squeeze to set it to work before sliding the garment up into place. It was of bright scarlet satin, boned and shaped to force her tits upwards and outwards, supporting but baring them. Helen had settled on a not-dissimilar garment in midnight blue, and turned her back on Malorie with a giggle.

'You lace me in first, then I'll do you,' she offered.

Malorie obliged her, then as the other girl tugged on the long laces of the red corset, she thought back to the last time she'd worn it, a week after Kinktastic.

~

Sinful Things was a new club, the promoters a couple who had recently moved down from Manchester, and it was packed the night Ricky and Malorie paid their first visit there. The venue, underneath a railway bridge, was divided into several separate zones, a mixture of chat and chill areas, two dancefloors, one of which had a stage for performances and, naturally, there was a dungeon area.

Malorie had recovered her equilibrium since the Master's wretched lecture at Kinktastic, and that night she was wearing her scarlet breast-baring corset with only the skimpiest scarlet panties, and high-heeled shoes with little rings on the heels that could be used to fasten her to something or hobble her – though Ricky would never do so in a new club, simply because they wouldn't know what the conditions underfoot were going to be like. He had his full leathers on; jeans, boots and waistcoat over a black silk shirt as well as black leather gloves. The pair of them had wandered round the venue in a leisurely fashion – at least, as leisurely as anyone could when the archways were often clogged with groups of people trying to see what thrills might await them in the next zone in either direction, had danced a little and had already decided not to watch the performance on stage at midnight. 'The usual crap, all short films of horses' cocks and car crashes, and some prat jumping about in body paint,' Malorie had remarked, making one or two people laugh and one or two others look mortally offended.

They were now sitting on one of the big squashy leather sofas in the main bar area, Malorie resting her legs across Ricky's lap. She spotted the Master, standing by the bar, surrounded by two or three male doms and Angela Curver, but there was no sign of the naked slave girl who usually accompanied him. She spilled some of her drink, and swore, quietly.

'What's up?' Ricky asked, then saw she was looking at the bald man, who was wearing an antique-looking dinner suit tonight and holding, as usual, a glass of brandy.

'Oh, bollock face over there? Fuck him. Well, don't, love, obviously.' Malorie giggled, feeling better, as Ricky leaned over to pull her closer to him. Whether or not the Master had heard, they never knew, but something attracted his attention to the Natural Born Thrillers. He took a sip from his drink and set it down before stalking purposefully towards them. Whatever he might have had in mind to say was forestalled by Ricky looking up at him and enquiring cheerfully, 'Where's your girlfriend tonight then? Dumped you, has she?'

'Do you make a fetish out of your lack of manners?' the Master enquired, but it was Malorie he was staring at. 'I fail to see what business it might be of yours.'

'Never mind, mate,' Ricky grinned, refusing to be in the least intimidated. 'You know what they say, every time you get chucked you learn what not to do next time. Life's full of learning opportunities, ain't it?'

The Master's eyes were still fixed on Malorie, but with Ricky's arm round her, she wasn't in the least disconcerted. The Master didn't appear to realise this.

'Learning opportunities are offered only to those worthy of them,' he said. 'All my slaves learn that much, at least. Once they are ready.'

At which Ricky, who had taken a mouthful of beer, snorted some down his nose – quite deliberately, Malorie thought – and shook his head at the Master. 'Oh, good line, mate. Good line. Practice in front of a mirror, do you?'

Malorie giggled at this point, unable to stop herself, and the Master snarled something inaudible and walked away. Ricky, blatantly losing interest in the man immediately, kissed Malorie long and hard, and gave her nipple a gentle pinch.

'Better?' he asked. She grinned. 'Much better. I feel like doing something horrible to someone. Someone other than you. How many miserable worms are there in the place tonight?'

'Oh, enough, I'd say.' Ricky glanced around. 'That one over there in the red posing pouch do you? Little Tim?'

'I'd say so, babe.' Malorie swung her legs down from his lap, got to her feet and advanced purposefully on the extremely submissive male who was cringing in happy anticipation as he saw her approach.

~

Those of the Master's guests who had stayed overnight were almost entirely male, including the pair of leather-clad non-conversationalists who had accompanied him to Kinktastic, and who were today behaving in a manner suggesting bodyguard or devoted paxman, though Malorie knew they were not actually part of the household. There were also one or two dom males Malorie had previously assessed as complete jerks. The only females apart from Helen and Malorie herself were two subbie girls, both blonde and pretty, who were with an American man Malorie had never met before., yet who looked somehow familiar. The American, who was tall and sandy-haired, with mature, clean-cut good looks, treated his two girls with a kind of playful sternness that appealed to Malorie: she hadn't seen much of this trio the night before, but watching them now gave her a pang of homesickness. Whatever the guests had been doing in the kitchen it hadn't been actual breakfast, because soon the maid brought in a trolley with a buffet of cold meats, bread, fruit and coffee. The American filled a plate with a selection of foods, handed it to the girls and told them to share: the other men in the room clearly expected both Helen and Malorie to wait on them and seemed to watch with a prickly insecurity which order they were served in. Malorie wondered initially if she or Helen should see that the Master was supplied with food first: glancing up at him she caught a momentarily baffled expression on his face, but he rapidly recovered himself and commanded Helen and herself to serve the guests. While this was being done, the Master strolled over to the window and gazed out at the windswept garden, commenting on the weather.

~

The Master was almost regretting having invited Lance Graham to his party. He had only met the American dom a couple of times, and only briefly, but he was aware that Graham had a high profile and a good reputation on both sides of the Atlantic. The Master had been sure that Graham would be interested in endorsing the Master's methods, but the other man had seemed more amused by the other guests than impressed. The Master was irritated: for all the awe he seemed to inspire, Graham didn't seem to have his two blonde cunts under particularly strict control. They answered him back, and giggled at some of his commands, yet he didn't inflict immediate punishment or even promise that it would be inflicted on a suitable occasion. Graham wasn't prepared to share them with anyone, either, which the Master thought poor form. He had put Helen at the disposal of all his guests, though he was not yet willing to allow anyone else to touch Malorie – for one thing, at this stage in her training, the cunt should be utterly frustrated at receiving neither pleasure or pain while all around her, others were being beaten, fingered and fucked. However, he did think it only right that he be allowed to use the cunts the other guests had brought along, ill-trained and unappealing as many of them were. When he turned back from the window, his thoughts in order, Graham had just poured himself a second cup of coffee and perched on the arm of the sofa where three of the other men were discussing the undesirability of fetish club dress codes. The Master strolled over, and indicated the American's two blondes, who were sitting on the floor some distance away, feeding each other pieces of fruit.

'Did it take you long to train them?' he asked, and Graham frowned slightly before replying.

~

Having served all those who wanted breakfast, Malorie wasn't quite sure what she was expected to do next. She glanced at Helen, who had retreated to a corner and was standing still, hands behind her back, her face composed. The Master was talking to that American bloke, and something about the posture of both men compelled Malorie's attention. Carefully, as naturally as she dared, she moved nearer to them, backing up to the wall and copying Helen's posture as much as she could. The Master was telling the American about his Method.

'In the correct combination, of course,' he said. 'Properly used and controlled, the right dosages open the mind, allow a woman to appreciate and accept her submissiveness. And the audioprogramming should be done every single night.'

A frown crossed the American's face. 'You sure that's fully safe, sane and consensual, my friend?'

Malorie held her breath and mentally went on her knees in gratitude to this man as the Master confirmed that, yes, he was talking about drugs and hypnosis. 'Only for those who want it, you understand,' he said. 'It takes a particular type of ... woman.' Malorie realised how close he had come to saying 'Cunt' and how he had realised that this would not, actually, impress the American dom at all. The other man shook his head slightly. 'So, what do you do if it doesn't work out?' he asked, and it was the Master's turn to frown. He obviously didn't want to admit that there was any chance of his Method failing, but eventually he sighed and said, 'Get rid of her, of course. Send her back to her friends. She regrets it, but she had her chance.'

'It's happened?' The American's question was noticeably pointed, and Malorie found herself wondering who this guy was, and what exactly he was up to. The Master frowned harder. 'Just the once. Stupid girl. She wasn't particularly... interesting in the first place. But she's of no consequence to me, now.'

He looked around, noticed Malorie and nodded to her.

'Coffee,' he said. 'For both of us.' Keeping her face as blank as she could, Malorie hurried to fetch more coffee, feeling as though the little audio recorder in the satin edging of her corset was glowing red hot. It had to be Indianna the Master was referring to, Indianna who had reportedly begun a relationship with him, dropped out of sight and later posted on SM Link that she was leaving the scene for the moment. Though Malorie didn't know the girl well, she had been concerned about her. This concern that was only partially relieved when a couple of customers she knew to be sensible enough mentioned having heard from Indianna briefly, that she was alive and well but just not interested in any kind of fetish socialising just now. Part of Malorie's concern had been down to seeing what both she and Ricky assumed was the Master's initial pickup of the girl, the same night Ricky had so gleefully slapped the man down.

~

Indianna had been looking unusually pretty, in a new white latex dress, buckled up the sides, very short and very low cut: Malorie had sold it to her the week before, and advised her that she shouldn't wear anything underneath it. 'Oh, and trim your muff, as well, or shave, I'd say,' she'd remarked, and Indianna had giggled.

Malorie had just rejoined Ricky at the bar after an enjoyable session with Little Tim, who had slavered ecstatically over her boots both before and after she'd strapped him to the A-frame and set about him with a wooden paddle and her diamante-handled riding crop, flicking his balls repeatedly with the tip of it then laying on a fine criss-cross pattern of welts over his flabby buttocks. She had sent him away happy, if sore, and made her own way back through the club. Ricky was buying her another rum and coke, so he didn't spot that The Master was about ten feet away from them, his hand on Indianna's shoulder. Malorie didn't say anything at first, not wanting to give Ricky the chance to ask her if she might be getting a little obsessed, but once he'd been served, Ricky turned round and saw the couple. Indianna was biting her lips and looked scared, but the Master wasn't letting go of her arm and was talking to her intently.

'Do you want to – ' Ricky whispered, and Malorie sighed. 'Maybe – Mm, maybe not.' She noticed that Indianna was smiling now, and though the smile was a nervous one, it carried some quality of excitement rather than distress, and she was nodding her head at something the Master said.

'Oh God, Ricky, I don't know,' Malorie whispered, moving in closer to him. 'Don't let me turn into one of those twatty dungeon monitors who can't leave anyone alone. Indianna's a big girl, and she knows lots of people here.' Even as she'd said it, she had a feeling she might regret her lack of intervention later, but at the same time, she was horny after her exertions, and reluctant to allow thoughts of the Master and whatever he might be doing to clutter up her mind any more than he had done already.

~

'Shibari isn't an area I've done much work in, of course,' The Master said, putting down his empty coffee cup. He was aware that some of the other guests were getting a little restive as so many of their slaves, being uncollared, untrained and in some cases, paid for their company at parties, had gone home. The atmosphere of any event with an overabundance of males tended to become difficult to manage if firm control was not rapidly taken. The Master had planned initially to use Malorie and Helen for some demonstrations of his Method, yet Lance Graham's attitude made him somewhat reluctant to do so: the American fool didn't seem to appreciate his ideas the way the Master would have expected him to. So, he might as well make use of the man in another way. Seeing the two pretty blondes elaborately bound in rope would be an entertaining diversion for the aspiring male doms, even if they weren't going to be allowed to touch. He carried on flattering Graham, and to his relief it wasn't long before the other man beckoned to one of his girls and told her to go and fetch the rope bag from the bedroom they had used. The other girl, without being bidden, picked up their breakfast plate and took it back to the trolley, then returned to the sofa where Graham had been sitting and stood by it, her hands clasped behind her back and her head bowed. Like her fellow subbie, she wore a little white satin slip and a pair of white satin high-heeled shoes. She was slender, with long straight fair hair, slightly bigger tits than the other girl and, as far as anyone could tell through the white satin, kept her pussy shaved smooth. The Master tried briefly to remember if he had seen enough of her to confirm or deny this the night before: he wasn't sure, but it wasn't particularly important. Graham went to her and removed the white slip in one smooth movement, baring her before them all and the Master saw that she was shaven.

The second girl reappeared, carrying a plain black cloth bag which she laid on the arm of the sofa. Graham turned to her, and made her as naked as the first girl, before extracting a bundle of soft, white rope and beginning.

He started by securing each girl's arms behind her back, before setting to work on an elaborate binding of the second girl's breasts. The Master, though he was not a particular fan of Shibari bondage, found himself appreciating the way the rope bit into the soft, tanned flesh. Graham repeated the pattern of loops and knots on the other girl, now and again tying off one rope and starting with another. The rest of the men in the room had drawn closer, and though some of them were commenting and conversing, they were doing so in low, appreciative tones. The Master glanced round them, saw that they were content, and returned his attention to Graham's two possessions. Both of them were breathing a little faster now and biting at their lips, both sets of tits rising and falling in their bondage. The Master felt a slight stirring in his cock; perhaps he would, at some point, devote some time to studying this particular speciality. Malorie, for instance, would make an impressive sight enmeshed in ropes, black ropes would be his preference, cutting cruelly into her skin. He took another look round the room and saw that Helen was standing by the fireplace, in the proper hands-behind-back position of a slavecunt awaiting instructions, but Malorie... Where was Malorie? He couldn't see her.

~

A few minutes into the American's shibari demonstration, Malorie had realised that no one was paying her any attention. Carefully, but casually and unhurriedly, she made her way towards the door, thinking that, should anyone say anything to her, she could claim a call of nature: the Master had never been particularly interested in fetishizing that aspect of his ownership. If that damned device of Ricky's had been working, she had the Master's own admission of unethical, unconsensual tricks on file, but even if it hadn't worked, there was the American. The American would be traceable, she was sure, and from the look on his face when the Master had outlined the core of his Method, the American would back up anything Malorie cared to say. It was enough: she could get out of here now. She could go home.

There was no time to dick around with trying to pack, which they had thought might happen and which was the reason why she'd brought only things she could happily abandon: she made it back to the wardrobe room long enough to grab a long black velvet skirt, presumably Helen's, and her own red PVC jacket. With these hurriedly pulled on over her corset, she would be able to pass as a Goth or something if anyone unconnected with the fetish scene saw her. She would not be arrested for public indecency, or stopped by the police and asked awkward questions. She wished fervently that she had thrown at least one pair of flat shoes into the bag she'd packed, but there was no time to fret about that now, she needed to hurry. She went quickly back down the corridor towards the kitchen, from which she knew a back door gave onto the back garden. This was reasonably well maintained but had a fanciful mini maze of hedges, which were rather overgrown. She had seen, through an upper window a couple of days ago, that beyond the maze was only a row of poplars, and she could get through those and out onto the main road which led down to a big coaching inn and a parade of little shops – and a phone box.

Just before opening the kitchen door, she paused, listening for the maid. The woman had some private room of her own, she must have. She didn't randomly roam the house and couldn't, surely spend all her time in the kitchen. There was no sound of her at all, so Malorie pushed the door a little and peeped round it, thinking she could make an excuse and bolt back to the dungeon if she had to – but the maid wasn't there. Malorie crossed the kitchen, her heart pounding and, she was surprised and almost amused to note, her pussy beginning to moisten with a massive adrenaline high. The back door gave a horrid creak as it opened, but she doubted the sound would carry far in this old, thick-walled house.

Outside, it was cold and blustery, shockingly cold after the indoor warmth, but Malorie didn't particularly care. She kept close to the side of the house, scuttled across the little terrace and into the hedge maze. The crazy-paved path between the hedges was mossy, and slippery, but Malorie had spent enough time crossing drink-drenched dancefloors in heels this high to be able to keep her footing. With every step, her sense of exhilaration and joy grew stronger, until she rounded a corner and ran almost full-tilt into one of the Master's leather henchmen.

'What do you think you're doing, slag?' he asked, almost conversationally, before picking her up and throwing her over his shoulder to march swiftly back towards the house.

CHAPTER SIX

Sundays, when Thrillers bothered to open, were always quiet, but this had to be the quietest Sunday on record, Ricky thought. He'd decided he might as well open up, as it would give him something to do. Given that Thrillers had a reputation for maybe-maybe not opening on Sundays, if punters did come, they often spent lavishly out of excitement and relief at not having had a wasted journey, but that old shopkeeper voodoo wasn't working today. He'd sorted out the previous day's delivery of a new range of books from an independent publisher with a nice line in femdom stories, and turfed out a couple of hoodie-wearing yobs who'd come in elbowing each other and asking where they could find some hot women who wore all that leather stuff, yeah? But since then, nothing had happened at all, and his thoughts were circling obsessively round and round the subject of Malorie and the Master. She'd said she'd be home within a couple of days, on Friday. She'd kissed him, one stolen kiss; he'd had his arms round her, felt the heat of her body, her mouth on his. Her hands had been cuffed, and he had cuffed her hands many times, tied her up, had her in any number of positions where she couldn't get away from him. And she'd done the same and more to him, time after time. He ached for her. She could walk in any minute and order him to drop to his knees and service her, or drag him upstairs and whip him, or strap him down and light the candles. She could walk in and he could grab her by her hair and throw her to the floor and fuck her, biting her tits and her throat with his cock deep inside her... And if he didn't stop thinking about her, he was going to break something. He had to stop thinking about her with the Master, being beaten and enslaved and owned by the Master, and maybe enjoying it, and maybe it was what she'd wanted all along, and maybe she'd forgotten all about Ricky and that was why he'd heard absolutely nothing. Or maybe the Master just wouldn't let her go. No one who had her would want to let her go. Ricky put down the rubberwear catalogue he'd been browsing, and shook his head. It really wasn't worth keeping the shop open this afternoon: he could close up, put a note on the door and spend the next few hours trawling the various websites and forums and chatrooms to see if anyone had posted anything about the Master: the girl who'd been in the shop on Friday had mentioned that it was a hot topic on the forums but hadn't gone into much detail. Maybe the baldy git had been bragging about having enslaved and taken Malorie. Maybe they were all talking about it still. He could just lurk, no one would know he was reading the stuff. No one online would be able to tell he was crying.

~

The shop door opened, the bell jangled. Ricky swallowed down his anguish and projected his amiable customer-service smile, which he let slip when he realised that it was Natasha Williams who had come into the shop. The dominatrix was uncharacteristically dressed down, in black jeans and a dark green knitted sweater, her magnificent red hair tied in a loose ponytail. She looked tired, and haunted, and her first words were 'Hi, sweetie, is Malorie in?'

He couldn't have been more shocked if she'd slapped him. Between the slightly awkward expressions of vague sympathy from regular customers, which had been mixed with an avid curiosity that had repelled him, and the comments from that pink-haired cutie about Malorie's alleged defection being all over SM-Link, he had formed the idea that absolutely everyone knew what was going on, or at least allegedly going on. This had been another factor that he and Malorie hadn't really planned out: how much other people would or should know while she was actually in the Master's hands.

How much Malorie had thought about what might occur in the online communities, he didn't know, as he had never been as interested in them as she was. Natasha, on the other hand, was a regular user of both SM-Link and Fetish Nation, the two biggest sites, yet she clearly didn't know what was happening. She was looking at him, a little oddly, and he realised he was standing there with his mouth open. He shook himself slightly, and said, 'She ain't here right now. Anything I can do for you, is there?'

Natasha bit her lip and lowered her eyes, and Ricky caught himself thinking it was an oddly subby move for her, but even in his misery, he couldn't help finding it slightly sexy. She lifted her head again and took a deep breath.

'I don't know. Oh hell. Can I – can I talk to you?'

He came out from behind the counter and put his hand on her arm. He liked Natasha, always had done, and there was clearly something very wrong.

'Look, it's dead today, let me close the door and then we'll go up to the flat and have a drink. Then you can tell me what's bothering you.'

~

Malorie was trying to collect her thoughts and work out exactly how much danger she was in. She had known that she risked unpleasant consequences if she was caught trying to get away – but if the Master worked out that she had planned to betray him all along, what the hell would he do to her? It had been bad enough already. The Master's henchman who'd caught her – and had he spotted her from a window, or was it just pure shitty luck that he'd appeared when he did? - had brought her back into the playroom, clapped his hand over her mouth just long enough for him to be able to put a gag on her – she had tried to resist but he had pinched her nostrils shut till she opened her mouth – and then he had cuffed her hands behind her back and fastened them to a ring in the wall.

'This looks like more fun for all of us,' he'd said cheerfully, and left the room. Malorie had been more frightened, then, than at any time since she'd first walked up the steps and knocked on the door of the Master's house. Part of the reason she'd made her bid for freedom when the house was full of people was because she doubted the Master would want to do anything blatantly non-consensual in front of witnesses, but this man had been there at Kinktastic and must have some idea of what the Master was really into. And now she was back in the dungeon, out of sight of the other guests. The American, at least, might have taken some notice if she had protested that she'd had enough and wanted to go, even if the rest of them were stupid and mean enough to at least pretend to believe that it was all part of the game. She yanked frenziedly at the ring her hands were fastened to but, of course, it didn't budge. The gag, a short stub of leather fastened through a leather strap, was making her drool; she tried to push it out of her mouth, but it wouldn't go, so she had to let the saliva spill down her chin. Eyes filling with tears, she craned her head round and tried to look at the cuffs on her wrists. They were heavy steel ones, probably illicitly-obtained police handcuffs and, though the man had not fastened them cruelly tight, there was no way she could slip a hand free. He'd used a padlock to attach them by their short chain to the ring in the wall, and taken the key to both that and the cuffs away with him. There was absolutely no way out. She sank defeatedly to her knees and tried not to cry, terrified that crying with the gag in place would stop her breathing.

~

Some time later, she heard voices and footsteps outside the playroom door: though the walls were thick, the door was less so, and did not fit perfectly into the frame. She couldn't clearly make out what was being said, but she could detect at least one female voice, which must mean one of the two submissive girls belonging to the American. She tried to scream and shout, but could only produce pitiful squeaks through the gag in her mouth and, after a moment or two, the voices dwindled away and she heard what had to be the sound of the front door opening and closing. Then footsteps rang loudly and clearly across the hall and the door to the playroom was thrown vigorously open.

~

Ricky took Natasha into the kitchen, made them both tea and got a half-bottle of whisky out to enliven the brew. He'd always been the more houseproud one so, even after more than a week without Malorie, the place wasn't a tip – not that he'd bothered much with cooking, or eating. Natasha didn't seem to notice, wrapping her hands round her mug as though she needed the warmth.

'What's wrong with you then, girl?' he asked when he'd poured a good splash of alcohol into his own drink. Natasha seemed to consider for a moment.

'Ricky, where is Malorie?' she asked.

'Like I said, she's not here right now,' Ricky repeated. He didn't know how much Natasha knew, but didn't want to lie to her – or tell her the truth. He waited, watching her visibly struggle with what she wanted to say, and seeing her distress made him want to set his own aside for the time being. Natasha took a deep breath. 'I heard this stupid rumour, but it doesn't make sense. But nothing is making sense at the moment. Nothing's been making sense since that fucking Kinktastic thing.' To Ricky's utter shock, Natasha Williams, the coolest, calmest, toughest dominatrix he'd ever met, dissolved into tears.

'Hey,' he said, 'Oh hey Natasha, come on, what the fuck is going on, what's the matter?' He got up and scooted round the table to sit next to her on the bench seat and put his arm round her; she dropped her head onto her own arms and sobbed for a minute or two.

'Oh shit, I'm sorry. I'm sorry Ricky. There's something awful going on, I really think there is. That guy. That arsehole who calls himself the Master. Malorie's not really with him, is she?'

Ricky took a deep breath, and tried to think about what he could safely tell her, but Natasha hadn't finished. 'If she is, I don't think she wants to be. There's something really wrong. There really is. Look, whatever he did at Kinktastic, it messed us all up. I thought he was full of shit, but ever since I went to that workshop of his, it's like I can't think straight. I've always been a top, ever since I first got into the scene, but now I can't stop thinking about going over. About letting him do things to me. I didn't want to tell anyone but I'm really in a mess about it. I can't even talk to Esmerelda, and you know I tell her everything, but I can't tell her this.'

Esmerelda, Natasha's favourite slave, was a decent, sensible person, whether she was in full winking, knowing, shemale maid mode or Les, 'her' daytime amiable male self, and a true friend of Natasha's along with the mistress-slave relationship they had. Ricky held her tighter, and understood properly, for the first time, what Malorie had seen and felt and realised about the Master, and why she had been so determined to do what she was doing. A mixture of rage and guilt flooded through him and he wanted to drive straight over to the Master's house, drag Malorie out of there and firebomb the place.

'He's a wanker,' he managed to say. 'Malorie knows what he is. What's he done to you, then?'

Natasha took a long, shuddering breath and pushed herself slightly away from Ricky.

'It's like I said. I can't stop thinking about submitting. I keep going over and over it and kind of wanting it, but I don't think I really want it. Oh shit, Ricky, that was why I came round here. I was going to talk to Malorie about it, because I knew she'd understand, before I said anything to you.'

'Well I'm sorry, girl, I'm really sorry she's not here. She's away for the moment,' Ricky said. 'But I'm here. You can talk to me if you want to, can't you?'

'That's it,' Natasha said. 'I wanted to talk to you. I wanted...' She stopped, and Ricky began to work out what she was leading up to. Despite his anger at the Master and his anxiety for Malorie, he felt his cock begin to harden as he understood. He remembered Malorie's near-frenzy after Kinktastic, and how she'd needed him, not the Master, to beat her and bring her to orgasm, to give her pain and then pleasure. But he had to be sure.

'Natasha, do you want me to top you? Is that what you want?'

Natasha shuddered. 'I don't know, Ricky, honestly. I don't know if it'll work. But I don't know what else will. It's been a couple of months and I can't get it out of my mind. And if it was you doing it, well, we're friends, aren't we? I trust you to stop if I want you to. And you won't hold it against me, or tell everyone, or anything.'

Even with everything else, even though he was almost consumed with his worry for Malorie and his longing for her, and his fury at the Master, Ricky couldn't help appreciating this for the compliment it was. There were plenty of male doms around who were good people, sure: superlatively skilled, or terrific company and generally well-liked. But he supposed few of them would really be able to resist letting it be known that Madame Natasha had bent over at last, even if it was only to their closest friends. Though Ricky was a switch and therefore had no problem with other people's opinions of whatever persona he was putting out on any given night, he didn't see anyone else's chosen roles as an opportunity for point-scoring: let 'em all do what they wanted when they wanted with who they wanted.

'You want to come through to the playroom, then?' he said. She nodded, slowly, and got to her feet.

~

The Master had been clearly in his element when he led the remaining male guests into the dungeon where Malorie was handcuffed to the wall, gagged and helpless. He'd made this dramatic speech about the danger of rebellion in slaves, and how it had to be punished harshly. Malorie had almost wanted to laugh at the absurdity of his performance until she realised, with utter terror, that this was a deliberate piece of theatre. He wasn't stupid enough to give any of these men the chance to panic about the ethics of his behaviour: by presenting it as a big, theatrical game, he was making sure that none of them would balk or feel guilty about what they were about to do to her. The hefty leatherman who had caught and chained her in the first place now moved over to her, bearing a nasty looking knife, and Malorie shrieked through her gag, but all he did was cut off her jacket and skirt and toss the ruined pieces into a corner, leaving her in nothing but her corset. Another man, who she now recognised as the Master's second henchman from Kinktastic, came up and undid the snap-ring that held her handcuffs to the larger ring cemented into the wall. Then the first man took a firm grip on her shoulders, lifting her slightly so that her feet had no purchase on the floor. Even if she'd thought to kick, or been fast enough, it was only seconds before the second man had hold of her by the knees, and the two of them were carrying her into the middle of the room. The first man let go of her, but the second seized her in a firm, disinterested embrace while his colleague went to a wooden item she had not previously experienced or seen in use. It was a slightly curved plane of wood with a couple of rings attached about halfway down the length, to which long chains were fastened. The man picked it up and brought it to where she was struggling in the arms of the other. He lifted her cuffed hands, dropping them over the length of the wooden shape as he held it against her. He then took a d-ring and passed it through the ring on her cuffs in order to secure her hands to the underside of this restraint board. The Master went to the side of the room and operated a switch so that two more chains began to descend from the ceiling: the two leathermen fastened these chains to the rings on either side of the thing, and then gave her a light push so that she fell forward and found herself helpless. She was riding the wooden board as though it were a swing but, with her hands immobilised, she couldn't get any purchase to get off it. One of the men then grabbed her flailing feet, slapped a leather restraint around her ankles and clipped it to another chain, which he then fastened to the ring in the wall, leaving her swaying and swinging on the wood, completely unable to free herself. She tried, even more frantically, to force the gag from her mouth, but it was impossible. The Master came to stand in front of her, smiling sadistically.

'You will love it,' he said. 'Whatever you think you might have been doing, this is what you really want, cunt.' He grabbed a handful of her silvery hair and twisted it round his fingers, pulling just enough to make her squeal round the gag. The Master turned his attention to one of his guests, a chubby man with thick lips and a faded t-shirt advertising a long-extinct fetish club. 'I think this would be an appropriate time to test that device of yours, Arthur,' he said. 'We didn't get a chance to use it last night, did we?' Chubby Arthur shook his head. 'Nah. The bird doesn't like it, so I don't put her in it. Safe, sane and consensual, and all that.' He said the last with a sneer that chilled Malorie before she remembered that the girl who'd been with him the night before had rather ostentatiously displayed that she was a professional, being paid for her time, and that she didn't think much of her assignment – though she had livened up when the American had offered to test a new single-tail on her. The Master smiled. 'Of course, Arthur. But when a cunt is properly trained, like this one is...' He yanked on her hair again and Malorie struggled to scream. 'She wants it. She wants whatever her Master chooses to do. She rebels only to be punished, and used in any way her Master sees fit to use her. And I see fit to use this one as a fuckhole. I think your new toy will be perfect for her.'

Arthur had already been rummaging in the bag he had with him, and now he brought out a weird-looking framework of steel and elastic bands. Despite her terror, Malorie recognised the basic shape of it from the time she and Ricky had stopped by the Bad Medicine stand at Kinktastic. That had been a stall selling all kinds of odds and ends which had a legitimate medical use but which could also be made into instruments of erotic torture. The thing Arthur was now approaching her with was a mutated, revamped version of a Jennings gag: something which would hold her lips apart and her mouth open, no matter what she did.

To fit it, they would have to take the gag off, Malorie realised, and frantically tried to formulate the right words to say, to scream, to make them let her go, but before she could do so, the leatherman standing behind her had removed the gag: she took one desperate breath and then Arthur had jammed the metal frame into her mouth, parting her jaws, pulling her lips wide open, and she could do nothing but grunt and whine.

The thing was not actually painful once in place. Arthur was clearly not a deranged sadist, but speech was going to be utterly impossible. The second leatherman took a firm grip on her head, one hand against each temple, after she tried to jerk herself out of reach, and Arthur, who didn't smell too pleasant, got placidly on with the job of fastening his device into place by looping and tying the bands behind her head and neck, and turning the ratchet to open her mouth as wide as possible. The Master had stood back while this was going on, smiling at her in a way that chilled her deeply. He wasn't angry with her: she could have understood that. He hadn't actually realised that she had deceived him, that she was spying on him. He was enjoying the chance to hurt and humiliate her; he thought that this was just a final spell of resistance on her part before ultimate surrender, and he was particularly glad that she had made what he considered a gesture of rebellion in front of other people.

The male doms, apart from Arthur, who was beside her, were all standing in a rough semi-circle behind the Master, and Malorie detected an odd undercurrent of awkwardness among them. Maybe some of them were actually getting the vibe that she wasn't happy, that this wasn't just a matter of the Master pushing a new subbie girl's limits. She knew them all by sight, though none of them more closely than as occasional customers and faces glimpsed in clubs, so it was probably safe to say that some of them knew her as the co-owner of Thrillers. The Master stepped back, sweeping out one arm in a grand gesture.

'An exquisite instrument, Arthur. Most effective, and quite elegant as well.' Arthur simultaneously smirked and shrugged. There was a further silence, broken only by Malorie's gurgled moans as she found some relief for her feelings in telling them what she thought of them all, even if it was in words which the device in her mouth rendered entirely incomprehensible.

'Arthur, perhaps you would care to demonstrate the procedure with this,' the Master said, picking up a large, black dildo of soft rubber from the shelf behind him. There was a tiny hint of exasperation in his voice and, for a second or so, Malorie found herself tempted to laugh. The Master had obviously intended to have all these wannabe tops fuck her mouth while she was in no position to resist but, either because they were put off by the wicked metalwork or because not one of them wanted to be the first to get his cock out, they were not rushing to volunteer.

Arthur seemed to draw himself up to his full height, taking in a long, loud breath through his nose as he took the dildo and came back to stand in front of Malorie. She thought, again, about resisting, but told herself that this might well make things worse. After all, she could handle having a dildo in her mouth. She didn't think this particular one had been up anyone's arse the night before and, even if it had, she did know that the Master was as fastidious about toy hygiene as anyone else on the scene. However, sucking a cock, whether flesh or silicone, was quite a different experience to having her face fucked when she was in no way able to resist, or control the thrusting. Luckily, Arthur was fairly tentative with the dildo, and didn't actually make her gag. However, she could glimpse, now and again, that a couple of the other men in the room were drawing nearer and starting to stroke their groins.

~

Ricky had decided to start by putting Natasha over his knee, and had, therefore, ordered her to strip. She had done so with a hesitant shyness that he found surprisingly erotic: in the past he had always been turned on by her cool, bitchy dominance. He sat in the straightbacked wooden chair, watching as she piled her clothes in the corner then came towards him, biting her lip. She was taller than Malorie, with big, pendulous, dark-nippled boobs and a lovely, creamy-white arse. He admired her for a moment, then drew her towards him and bent her over his lap. Her long, red ponytail brushed the floor and she braced herself on her hands, straddling her legs slightly. He stroked the curve of her buttocks, admiring the soft skin, completely unmarked by whip or cane, or even a handprint. He raised his hand and gave her one firm spank, medium strength. She let out a little gasp, and he did it again. He paused, then, but she said nothing and made no attempt to pull away from him, so he resumed the spanking, alternating between smacks on each cheek and on the tops of her thighs, stroking her arse now and again to feel the warmth of her flesh as it reddened under the blows. She began to whimper, then to moan, lifting her feet in turn, and Ricky felt his cock hardening.

'Stand up,' he said, keeping his voice calm and even, and she obeyed. Her face was as flushed as her rear, and her eyes bright as though she might be about to cry, but she didn't ask him to stop.

'Over the whipping stool,' he said. 'Legs apart.'

When she was in position, he selected a light, thin, whippy cane from the rack and flexed it a couple of times. It would sting, but wouldn't leave too much of a mark, as long as he was careful. He took careful aim and let fly, and Natasha squealed.

'Ohh! Ow! Jesus!'

Ricky laid on another stroke, then paused. 'That's two,' he told her, perhaps unnecessarily. 'Can you take four more? Six of the best should do you, shouldn't it?'

'No – Yes. Oh God, OK, yes,' Natasha moaned, her voice cracking. She would be crying by the final one, Ricky reckoned, and it would either have worked, or it wouldn't have. He didn't rush the next four, but didn't keep her waiting too long, either, and when he said, 'Six. Get up,' she turned round to face him, sobbing, and clapped her hands to her abused behind, but she was half-smiling through her tears.

'Thank you, Ricky,' she choked, and he took her in his arms, stroking her hair and murmuring to her, soothingly. He felt better in himself, as well. Somehow, this little encounter had taken away some of the desperate anguish he felt over Malorie; given him more confidence that she would be back beside him soon.

'I should thank you properly,' Natasha said, suddenly, and dropped smoothly and gracefully to her knees. 'Shouldn't I?' She was reaching for the fastening of his jeans and Ricky, his cock throbbing, didn't resist when she undid the zip and delved inside.

She was not the most skilled cocksucker he had encountered, but he didn't care: she probably didn't do it very often, yet she was trying her best. Between his pent-up need for release and the thrill of having topped Madame Natasha, it took very little time for him to come, and he only realised as he did so that she had her free hand between her legs, and was rubbing her clit hard and fast so that, as he slipped out of her mouth she tipped her head back and tensed briefly in an orgasm of her own.

CHAPTER SEVEN

Munches were an aspect of the fetish scene that Malorie and Ricky had not bothered with much since the opening of Thrillers, though they sometimes dropped in with flyers if they had a special event they wanted to promote. The Sunday Comedown one, held fortnightly at a pub a bare ten minutes' walk from the shop, was the one they were most likely to attend, but neither of them had been for months. When Natasha suggested it, though, Ricky was initially reluctant.

'Nah, you go if you feel like it.' He'd grinned, despite himself. 'Feeling better now, are you?' She was dressed again, and they were back in the kitchen, drinking whisky with water rather than tea. Natasha smiled and picked up her glass.

'Definitely. Thanks, Ricky. Oh but, look – where is Malorie? It's not true about her and the Master, is it?'

'Depends what you mean by true,' Ricky said, before he could stop himself. Natasha stared at him, shocked.

'Oh, God, Ricky, have you two split up? And I came here with all my problems and bullshit, oh, shit, I'm so sorry.'

'It's OK, don't be sorry.' Ricky didn't want her to feel bad. 'Come on, it's always good to see you. Even more, now.' Natasha been affected by the Master, had reason to hate him. She would understand, probably more than most. Also, she had trusted him with her own feelings, her own issues with the man: now it was time to trust her. He knew, fundamentally knew, that Malorie would feel exactly the same.

'She's gone to his place to stitch the little tosser up,' he said, quite calmly. 'She reckoned if she pretended she'd fallen for him, she'd be able to find out what the fuck he's doing, because it's not just being Mr Big Dominant, he's up to something.'

'Oh, my God.' Natasha looked stunned, then delighted. 'Bloody hell, good for Malorie. So, what's she doing, how long's she been in there?'

So Ricky outlined the plan, such as it was: the sound recorders, the little cameras. Malorie's late-night presentation of herself on the Master's doorstep, and her reappearance in the shop two days ago – and how little he actually knew about how his lover was faring in the Master's house. Natasha was enthralled, but then even keener to take Ricky along to the Sunday Comedown.

'He never goes to munches, but some of those dickhead wannabe doms do... I heard he was having one of his parties last night, so there might be some news, or at least some gossip. Oh, come on, come with me.'

'All right,' Ricky conceded. He was feeling better for having told someone – and, if he was honest, he was feeling better for having topped someone, made her scream, come in her mouth...The token spanking he'd given that silly pink-haired girl on Friday had been a brief relief of tension, but not enough for him. He also felt a need for company, friendly company: the flat was echoingly, miserably lonely without Malorie.

'Let me change my shirt, and we'll go.'

He could take his mobile with him. Malorie would ring once she was safely away from the house. He wouldn't drink any more, so he could go and get her, straight away, if he had to.

~

'She'll be better for a beating,' the Master said, as Arthur withdrew the spit-soaked dildo from Malorie's mouth for the last time. He was determined to retain control over the proceedings, and he had become aware that the men were too hesitant to fuck the cunt's face in front of each other. Silently, he despised them while understanding that they were the core market for his Method. He looked at Malorie, looked into her frantic eyes, and relished the sight of her face distorted by the adapted Jennings gag, wet with drool;

her hands jerking as she tried to work out some way of freeing herself from the restraint board. She moaned, and he felt his own cock harden. He picked up a medium-weight, rubber flogger and handed it to the nearest guest, a slender red-haired account handler from Birmingham. 'Warm her up, Jerry,' he said. Jerry's first blow with the flogger brought a squeak from her, rather than a full-blooded scream, but the man had laid it on quite lightly. The Master reminded himself to be patient: it would be more effective for the beginning of the beating to be close to erotic for the cunt, as well as the aftermath. Whatever she thought she'd been doing, she would be entirely broken after this, entirely his. Jerry thrashed her arse several more times, bringing it to a rosy glow of warmth, and then stepped back, and the Master handed a shorter, thinner-tailed flogger to another guest and invited him to continue the proceedings.

~

The pub was called the White Swan, and was the sort of place that was generally deserted on a Sunday evening, hence its popularity as a munch venue – and the munch crowd's popularity with the landlord. When Ricky and Natasha walked in, the back bar was at least half-full of people engaged in animated conversations. Little Miss Pink Hair was there, and Ricky was half-amused, half-embarrassed to see that she lit up at the sight of him, but her face fell when

Natasha put a hand on his arm and asked him what he wanted to drink.

'Coke, please, girl, just in case I have to drive later,' he said. He'd had a couple of whiskies at the flat, but that was all. While she went to the bar, he made his way up to a group round the nearest table, which included Harry and Cath Nicholas, both of whom looked slightly awkward when he drew level with them, and he supposed they might have been talking about him and Malorie. Harry, certainly, was a shocking gossip and Cath wasn't far behind him, but the pair of them were rarely malicious.

'Long time, no see, mate,' Harry observed, and Ricky nodded, then smiled, politely and hopefully not too miserably: his stomach was suddenly churning. What was he going to do if anyone asked him, outright, about Malorie? Lie, he supposed, and hope that they would be forgiven when the truth came out. He quickly tried to divert the conversation to what the Nicholases had been doing lately, which did hold them for a while as they had recently been to a notorious and very expensive holiday resort in the Caribbean, for the place's annual International Fetish Week. When they were interrupted by another friend, Ricky stepped back, sipping his coke, watching Natasha lay down the law to a pair of frequently cheeky maids – dressed in boyswear tonight, of course. He noted that the infernal Angela Curver was there, talking intently to a big, rather good-looking bloke who Ricky thought was vaguely familiar. Then he heard the man say, 'Honey, I think you're misguided,' in an unmistakeably American accent, and tried not to show surprise. Surely that was Lance Graham. Ricky wished he had known that Graham was coming over to England: he could have suggested the man do a ropework demo in the shop, invited customers only, or something. This was followed by the painful thought that Lance Graham's visit had probably been all over the internet forums and, if Malorie had been home, she would have known about it.

Just then, he heard her name mentioned by Angela, and sighed: when it was followed by his own, and a finger pointing in his direction, he straightened up and moved over to where they were standing.

'Oh,' Angela said, and seemed disconcerted: Ricky nodded at her and smiled at the American, wondering, rather meanly, what Angela would do.

'Hi,' said Lance Graham. 'I think I was just hearing about you. You run a shop, right?'

Ricky said that he did, and that he stocked a couple of books which featured Lance and his girls.

'Didn't know you were coming over here, to be honest,' he said. Lance frowned. Almost abruptly, he asked, 'You know that guy? The Master? What do you make of him?' Ricky understood with a sudden delighted surprise, that Lance Graham had not only been informed that Ricky's girlfriend had left him for the Master, but that Lance Graham didn't think much of the Master, whatever Angela thought. Angela butted in at this point.

'Lance and I were at the Master's last night, actually. We saw Malorie. She's looking well, Ricky. Is she still involved in the shop?'

Ricky was reminded, once again, exactly why Malorie had despised this woman. He had to swallow before he answered, 'Well, yeah.' Then he couldn't think of anything else to say.

Lance, who also gave the impression of not being overly fond of Angela, now looked her up and down with a gaze that wasn't particularly friendly. 'Angela, honey, have you ever bent over for the Master?'

'I was there last night, you saw me!' she said, and Lance frowned.

'Yeah, you were there. But I didn't get the impression you'd gone through his training programme,' he said. 'Is it not your kink?' Angela looked from one to the other of them, and licked her lips.

'It doesn't matter,' she said. 'Everyone's kink is different.' She glanced around, set eyes on a couple of obvious newbies and said, 'Anyway, nice talking to you,' and moved away. Ricky and Lance looked at one another, and then Lance said, 'I hear your girl left you, for him. How are you feeling about that?'

~

that it was Ricky and their friends, playing with her like this: she would hold that thought, no matter what they did next. She kept her eyes shut, not even really hearing the muttered conversations going on around her.

Suddenly there was a hand at the back of her neck and she squealed, despite herself, but what was happening was the removal of the gag.

'Of course,' the Master was saying. 'You are all welcome to come back again for further mentoring, but I regret that we have to draw this event to a close.'

Malorie was so far away in her own imagination that it took her several seconds to realise what was happening. Arthur was taking his device off her in order to go home, and the rest of the various would-be doms were leaving. She tried to collect her thoughts enough to say something, to ask them to take her with them, but her mouth was unresponsive, her lips uncontrollably floppy after the gag.

'No, we'll leave her, I think,' the Master said, calmly, as he ushered his guests towards the door. 'She can learn patience.'

Malorie raised her head, watching them all file out, and found herself looking directly into the Master's eyes. She wondered, for a moment, what he was thinking, but he shook his head, turned out the light and closed the door, leaving her still suspended in the darkness.

Malorie had been beaten by all the men no thought. Her arse was hot and throbbing, there hot, throbbing places across her upper bac shoulders, too, and between her legs was a v heat. She had decided, early on, that the best v endure the pain was to eroticise it: to turn it i safe fantasy in her mind. She had sometimes ti to Ricky about being the victim of multiple fac sadists – he had agreed that he, too, somet wanted to be put through such an ordeal. For bo them, though, the scenario culminated in having other one there, perhaps to deliver the final clim pain, perhaps to rescue them and finish performance in a tender ecstasy of lovemaking the thrashing progressed, she had closed her eyes, better to imagine that it was Ricky: either wield the whip or cradling her face and whispering d secrets to her.

And now, suddenly, it had stopped. She was s helplessly chained to the board, swaying gently a swung in the chains, her face still distorted by t metal frame that held her mouth wide open, but t men had all stepped back away from her. Her s pulsed: she wanted something inside her, but not ju anyone, or any random dildo: what she wanted w Ricky. She almost wanted Ricky to fuck her mout through the Jennings gag, pull her hair and come a over her face: if it was Ricky, it would be good. Sh had been pretending, all the way through the beating

~

It didn't take many minutes for Ricky to realise that he could trust Lance Graham with the truth. The American clearly had no time for The Master – and, to Ricky's delight, had actually heard the Master admit the truth about his Method.

'Goddamn hypnotic audiotapes, and giving girls drugs, what an asshole. Even if it is fifty percent bullshit, what a stupid asshole. But, listen, if you want to get your lady back, I reckon the effects would wear off pretty quickly, once she found out what he's actually doing to her.'

'She knows, though.' Ricky said. He took one quick glance around: no one was paying them any particular attention. Nosy many of them might have been, but few were brash enough to barge in on what must look like a very private conversation.

'Malorie's in there to find out what he's up to. She doesn't really want to be with him.' Even though he knew it was true, that it had to be true, it still hurt a little to think about the possibility of it not being true. He swallowed, and went on. 'She's got some sound recorders and things with her, she's trying to get evidence of what he's actually doing, and then we're just going to blow the bastard out of the water with it. But if you've heard him say it, and she's seen him do it, then that should be enough.'

Lance grinned. 'Oh yeah. But we can get a third, you know. Ever met a girl called Indii Livingstone? She knows all about that asshole, as well.'

'Indianna?' Ricky asked. 'Oh, God, yes. It was partly what happened to her that set Malorie off. She went off with the Master and the next thing was, she was right off the scene, and wouldn't talk to anyone.' Realising he was at the risk of sounding uncaring, he added, 'Do you know if she's OK?'

'Sure she is. She just didn't think anyone would believe her, at first, or at least they'd say she asked for it, or got him all wrong, you know how it goes. So I thought if I came over and nosed around, you know, got to know the guy a bit, I could tell her what I thought, and maybe tell a few other people if I found out stuff people ought to know, you dig?'

~

Ricky dug. He thought back to the last night before Malorie left: lying in bed with her, talking it all through, yet again. They'd come up with a variety of scenarios, previously: pretending to quarrel in a club and then Malorie letting the Master approach her to offer comfort; Malorie phoning the man and asking to see him privately – but they hadn't been sure that any of these would pan out. Malorie remained convinced that the Master had done something to her, and probably to the other women who had been

there, during his workshop at Kinktastic, and kept saying that this had to be something she could use.

'All that stuff about how we'd know if we were ready, we'd admit it to ourselves. I think it's some kind of hypnotic suggestion, but it doesn't work quite as well as he thinks.'

'But he reckons it works, so he'd not be that suspicious if you did go up and ask him to do you, would he?' Ricky had mused. Finally, Malorie had thought of turning up on his doorstep late at night, claiming she hadn't been able to help herself. It had appealed to Ricky, from a dramatic point of view, as well.

The spyware they had found on the internet was all tested and ready to go. Tomorrow, Malorie was going to do a thorough stockcheck on the shop, and sort out as much paperwork as possible then, after dinner, Ricky would drive her to the Master's house. He wasn't looking forward to that part.

'I'll miss you,' he said, very quietly, holding her close. 'Take care of yourself in there, won't you?'

'Oh, Ricky, love, I'll miss you as well,' she murmured. Her leg slid in between his and she started to kiss his face and then his chest. 'It won't take long. I don't want to stay there any longer than I have to.'

He felt himself growing hard, his cock unfurling against her thigh. She pushed him gently onto his back and straddled him, sitting up astride him, so he reached for her breasts and began to play with the nipples, gently pinching and teasing them. Her pussy was open and wet against the length of his cock, sliding to and fro, but she hadn't put it inside her yet; she was teasing herself with it, and teasing him, knowing how much he wanted to feel her hot sex enclosing him but making him wait, making herself wait. He groaned, and closed his eyes for a moment, then opened them again, wanting to look at her, not wanting to miss a second of this.

'Ready?' she whispered.

'Oh, God, yes, baby, yes!'

She rose up a little, took him in her hand then sank down, guiding him in, juicy lips sucking at his rod, and he squeezed her tits, holding his breath tensing his muscles so he didn't come straight away, and she started to ride him. They hit a shared rhythm straight away, hard and fast; his hands dropped to her hips, gripping them and rocking her backwards and forwards as she bounced on his cock, squeezing him with her cunt walls, saying his name again and again, stroking his cheek with one hand while she fingered her clit with the other, gazing down at him, holding the eye contact and, just when he thought he couldn't take any more, a great shudder rippled through her as she came, and he let himself go, shooting inside her with a cry of joy, wishing he'd never have to let her go.

~

Lance was looking at him a little quizzically, and Ricky wondered if he'd been noticeably lost in his thoughts. He gave himself a mental shake and said, 'Do you think Malorie knew you were there? Did you speak to her?'

Lance considered for a moment. 'I didn't get to talk to her, or the other one. He had them both doing maid stuff, and no permission to speak. Your lady looked OK, like she was keeping it together. Going by what Indii told me, if she knows what she was getting into, she should be all right. Hey, look, I was going to go see Indii this evening, anyway, and tell her what I thought about that guy. You want to come along? I tried to get her to meet me here, but she didn't feel like it, so I said I'd drop in later.'

Natasha appeared, at precisely that moment, and looked from one to the other of them before smiling at Lance and saying, 'Mr Graham, nice to see you.' Lance greeted her politely, then paused, and Ricky said quickly, 'Natasha knows the score here. But she's the only one who does.'

~

Though Lance Graham offered to pay for a cab, Ricky said he'd rather drive, so they walked back to the shop to get the car. Lance and Natasha chatted about mutual friends, a conversation they continued in the back of Ricky's Vauxhall as they drove to Indianna's place. Though Ricky knew most of the people the others were discussing, he didn't join in the chat. He was beginning to regret accepting Lance's invitation, and wondering if he shouldn't simply be heading straight for the Master's house to get Malorie out of there, now there were two separate witnesses to what the short-arsed bastard's famous Method actually involved. He patted his jacket pocket, checking his phone was there: if she called him now, he'd be off like a shot, never mind what his passengers might think about it.

~

Indianna Livingstone had been wondering whether she shouldn't have gone to the munch, after all. She was beginning to feel that bailing out of the whole fetish scene, after one unpleasant experience, was simply cutting off her nose to spite her face. Even if she did get asked a lot of nosy questions, by people who had heard one rumour or another, it wouldn't be the worst thing that ever happened. She was glad that Lance Graham was coming over later: perhaps he would bring her some other scene gossip as well as a rundown on what he thought of the Master. She suspected Lance and the Master wouldn't take to each other very well. Even though some people said that all the male doms tended to stick together when it came to whiny subs who topped from the bottom, when she'd told Lance, in a series of emails, about her night in the Master's house, he had been gratifyingly outraged on her behalf.

'Honey, this guy gives the rest of us a bad name right... I am gonna fly to the UK next month anyway, will see if I can't check him out and maybe tell him what a real Top does,' he had written, and Indianna, blushing as she read the message, had felt the first stirrings of renewing desire to submit again. But the next time she did it, she would choose someone who she could trust. She had never actually been involved with Lance in any sexual or BDSM fashion: their friendship was mostly Internet-based. On the few occasions they had met, though, she had felt there was a bond of goodwill between them. She was looking forward to his visit this evening and was surprised, and not entirely pleased, to find that he had brought Ricky Smith and Madame Natasha along, as well. However, when Lance explained in a few short sentences that Natasha and Ricky were as keen to see the Master get his come-uppance as Indii herself was, she found it was no hardship to tell them what had happened to her.

~

It hadn't seemed too bad at first, although she hadn't appreciated the Master addressing her as 'Cunt' in front of the taxi driver taking them back to the Master's house. Even when they were inside the house, and he had thrown her down to her knees and told her that she would only belong to him if she could prove herself worthy of it, she had found it more exciting than anything else.

He ordered her to crawl to his playroom: she obeyed, and then followed his instructions to strip and bend over the whipping stool. He'd used a single-tail on her, steadily, for quite some time and brought her off with his hand to finish the session, but had neither commanded nor permitted her to do anything to gratify him, which she had found slightly strange. Then he had asked her what she thought of his Kinktastic performance, and when she confessed that she hadn't been there, he'd seemed irritated. Within a few minutes, however, he quite deliberately appeared to change his mood. He'd used an intercom to summon a maid with drinks, given her a drink, and then told her she might sleep in the room off the dungeon.

Indii had been slightly put out by this, especially as she found a pair of high-heeled shoes and a suspender belt by the side of the bed, once the Master had left the room. But the thing that had really creeped her out had been waking in the night to hear what sounded like his voice calling her, as she thought, a worthless cunt who needed to learn her place. She had wanted to protest but found that she was too disorientated to do anything much, at which point she worked out that he must have drugged the drink he'd given her. His voice continued, muttering unpleasant suggestions, for quite some time before she went back to sleep.

She wasn't entirely clear about what had happened the next morning, only that it had been upsetting, and then she had been put in a car driven by some bloke she didn't know and driven back to the bus station on the edge of town.

~

'Audiohypnosis,' Ricky said when she finished her story. 'He's playing tapes he's made, recordings, while the girls sleep. And drugs, yeah. He's drugging girls.'

'I know,' Indianna said, a trifle crossly. 'Lance believes me, don't you, Lance?' The American nodded. 'Sure I do, honey. The asshole said as much himself- and now your girl - ' he looked across at Ricky. 'Well, she knows, cos he's done it to her, too. Even if she hasn't got it on tape, there's what she's had done to her, and what he said to me, and what he did to Indii here.'

'So, what are we going to do about it?' Indianna asked, and Ricky got to his feet.

'What I'm going to do is get Malorie out of there,' he said. 'And we're both going to tell him what we fucking think of him, aren't we?'

'Both of you? How about all of us?' Natasha put in. 'He might not have had me in his dungeon, but he fucked with my head, too. Don't forget that.'

Indianna looked at her in some surprise, but Natasha didn't elaborate, and the other girl shrugged slightly, but accepted it, and picked up a coat from the back of an armchair,

'I'm up for that,' she said. Lance pulled out his mobile. 'I sure am – just let me call the girls.' When Ricky grimaced slightly, he added, 'Just to tell them I'll be back late – my two subs stayed in the hotel tonight, they were tired. He didn't get anywhere near them, so we can leave them out.'

He was dialling as he spoke, and in the general bustle of leaving Indii's house, Ricky noted only that he kept the conversation short, and spoke firmly to whoever answered the phone, but for all the dominant-male manners, he was clearly respectful and affectionate towards his girls. Got to remember, Ricky thought, not everyone who's a one-way top is a dickhead.

CHAPTER EIGHT

Malorie heard the dungeon door open and screamed: she couldn't help it. It was more of a yelp than a full-blooded scream, but she was still a little ashamed of herself, particularly when a low light came on and she heard Helen's voice calling her name.

For the first time since she had made her bid for freedom, she remembered Helen, and wondered what the other girl had been doing throughout that long afternoon and evening. It occurred to her, as it hadn't done before, that while Helen spent a lot of her time either in the dungeon with Malorie or doing the various domestic tasks that both of them had been assigned, there had been considerable chunks of time where Helen had not been around, yet Malorie had never really given it much thought. She began to shiver, again, suddenly aware that she knew very little about Helen and her real role in the Master's household. In the hierarchy of slaves, where did Helen stand?

~

Helen had, in fact, had rather a dull afternoon after Lance Graham's rope bondage demonstration. Towards the end of it, Kevin, one of the Master's two closest friends, had come and taken the Master to one side for a whispered conversation, shortly after which, while Graham was untying and joking with his girls, there had been something of a change in the atmosphere. Helen was accustomed to simply accepting any instructions the Master gave her: that was her function as his slave. Having accepted that he was the Master and therefore in charge of the situation, to see him seemingly not fully in control, surprised and put out by something, worried her a little. However, she assumed that it must have been something that Lance Graham had said or done, because the Master had indicated, without any rudeness, that the American might like to think about leaving now. Graham and the two subbies had done so, quite happily. At this point, it had occurred to Helen that she hadn't seen Malorie for a while, and she had considered asking permission to seek out the other girl. Before she could work out the correct way to frame such a request, though, the Master had summoned the maid – Helen, like Malorie, had never been able to discover the woman's name, nor ever had any conversation with her other than utterly functional – and then beckoned to Helen.

'You have had enough entertainment, cunt. Now it's time to make yourself useful. Do as you are told.' From which Helen understood that the maid was going to assign her some domestic tasks, which was indeed what happened as the Master escorted the remaining guests downstairs. As she fetched and carried, cleaned and polished, Helen vaguely assumed that Malorie was, currently, the object of the other men's attention: well, Malorie had not been called on to submit in any particular way the night before, so it was probably only fair. But, when the housework was done, Helen was somewhat disappointed to be simply left in the sitting room, with no company and no amusement. For the first few minutes, she expected the Master to reappear, or at least to summon her via one of the bells or intercoms, or even by means of a message via the maid, but nothing happened.

Helen waited for some time in the middle of the room, head bowed and hands clasped behind her back, anticipating that, at any minute, someone would come to fetch her, or that they would all come back to make use of her, but when nothing at all happened, she found the confidence to step out of the slave posture and look around her for a book to read, at least. She was glancing along the bookshelves, wondering if there would be any difference in the Master's attitude depending on what he found her reading, when she heard voices and movement downstairs, which she was able to decode as the Master bidding guests farewell. Returning to her original posture of submissive anticipation, she waited.

The Master stalked back into the room, stripped to the waist and glowing with excitement. He made for the cupboard and poured himself a brandy, which he drank in one gulp. Then he breathed deeply, and turned to look at Helen, running his eyes up and down her body.

'Well, cunt. Have you been useful?' he asked. With a shiver, Helen murmured that she had.

'Be more so,' the Master said, and unfastened his trousers. 'On your knees,' he told her, and Helen went down immediately. He crossed the room and, grasping his cock in one hand, slapped it slowly across her face a couple of times.

'Open your mouth.'

Quivering with excitement – this was not a service she was often permitted to perform – Helen parted her lips and extended her tongue, tentatively licking at the head of the Master's phallus. He clasped his hands behind his back and stood perfectly still, looking down at her: she risked one glance upwards then devoted herself to the task, licking and sucking, getting the shaft thoroughly wet with her saliva before sliding her mouth down the length of him, taking the hot organ in as deeply as she could and swirling her tongue around it. She used the tips of her fingers to caress his balls as she sucked, getting into a comfortable, steady rhythm, feeling the cock pulse and swell in her mouth. She was aware of his breathing speeding up, and began to ready herself for the moment he would go still, orgasming without spurting, as was his preferred way of proceeding. To her surprise, a surprise she only just managed to conceal, the Master gave a low shout, pulled out of her mouth and proceeded to spray hot jizz over her face and chest. She stayed still, closing her eyes, waiting to see what would happen next. The salty drops trickled down her cheeks, rolled onto her breasts, and the Master said nothing for several moments. She heard him take a step back.

'Clean yourself up,' he said, unemotionally. 'Then go and attend to the other cunt. She's been restrained long enough to have learned her lesson. I shan't be needing either of you tonight, so you will remain in the dungeon till the morning.' Helen waited for a moment more, and the Master took hold of her hair and pulled her upwards, so that she scrambled to her feet, eyes wide open in mild shock, with an odd thrill running through her. The Master was rarely predictable, and it crossed her mind that his manner now might indicate that some new level of her training was about to be reached.

'Go.' He ordered her, and turned away, clearly intending to get another drink. Helen swiftly did as she was bid, hurrying out of the room and making for the stairs.

~

The Master drank his brandy and glanced round the room: it was in excellent order, as he would have expected. The maid would have ensured that Helen – and Malorie, had she not been otherwise engaged – performed all the necessary housework correctly before she retired to her own private suite of rooms on the second floor. The Master allowed himself a small smile. He had no sexual interest in the maid whatsoever: their arrangement had a financial basis and was satisfactory on both sides. The maid, in return for free board and lodging, and the chance to live out her own elaborately detailed fantasies about hierarchy and gracious living, was the perfect servant, with a servant's knack of absenting herself when there were things taking place that she didn't want or need to see.

Helen, too, understood her role and her position: she was the greatest success of his Method so far. When he had been living in America, there had been other girls, for a short time at least, but they had tended to prove unsatisfactory after a while. Online, a great deal of gratification was available, but the potential for disappointment when a meeting was finally arranged often deterred him from taking the extra step. However, the past few months had helped him consolidate his position, he felt. It was a pity about that girl he had begun the Method on during the one weekend Helen had gone to visit her elderly grandmother. She had proved unsatisfactory but, then again, Helen had returned a better slave than ever. That Malorie had tried to leave... well. It would have been the last struggles of the landed fish, the final panic before accepting the need to surrender. Now she would understand that she was broken, that she was his, and he would be able to use her as an example to others, just like Helen.

He wondered for a moment or two if he should have told Kevin and Robert to stay a little longer: they, at least, would have enjoyed making use of Malorie while she was bound and available to them, and wouldn't have been as squeamish as some of the guests. But no, it was more satisfactory to have both her and Helen to himself this evening. The Master threw himself on the sofa and stretched out: a short rest, and then he would allow himself the enjoyment of taking the pair of them.

~

Helen had untied Malorie and led her into the sleeping space, murmuring soothingly, just as she had done on Malorie's first night at the Master's house. Malorie let her, not saying anything, her mind racing. Helen always seemed happy to submit to the Master, content to belong to him, and had more than once encouraged Malorie to simply accept his dominance and revel in it. Malorie wondered if there was any way in which Helen might be jealous of Malorie, and resent sharing the Master's attentions with her, or if she could be made to feel that way and therefore want Malorie gone?

Helen helped her to sit down on the bed, letting her take her weight on one hip rather than on her poor, abused, backside. Malorie took a deep breath. Her face felt almost normal again, and she hoped she would be able to speak properly.

'Helen, are you really happy here?' she asked. The other girl looked at her blankly and then bit her lip: still, Malorie could tell that her own speech was almost back to normal and that Helen was simply disconcerted by the question.

'Oh yes,' she sighed. 'This is what I always wanted, a real Master. You wanted it too, didn't you?' Now it was Malorie's turn for a blank look, and a moment's jolted unease: did Helen suspect something off-key? But Helen had more to say.

'He always says, he knows what you need, he knows that lots of women need a Master to take control of them, they just need to understand and accept it. But only a few of us are really worth his time, he says. There are going to be more of us soon, now more people understand.'

For the first time in an hour or more, Malorie remembered the little sound recorder stitched into her corset, and wondered if it was still working, or whether it had been damaged by a stray blow from a whip or quirt or crop. What Helen had to say might be more evidence to use against the Master when she got out of here. 'Do you think people will understand how his Method works?' she asked, carefully, not sure how much Helen herself understood what must have been done to her. Helen frowned.

'Well, you know, it's something they have to learn,' she said. 'We're still in training, but we're understanding more of it all the time. He says other Masters can learn from him, but only if they're prepared to... To accept his teaching.'

Pay for it, you mean, Malorie thought but didn't say. She realised that she was feeling sharper than she had done in several days: the prolonged beating, coupled with the adrenaline rush of her failed escape, must have broken the influence of the Master's drugs and tricks. Suddenly it seemed very important to get it across to poor, bemused Helen that the way the Master had been treating both of them was wrong and unfair.

'Have you been with many other masters, then?' she asked. Helen looked at the floor.

'No, not really. I did a bit online, trying to find the right one, but it was... I don't know, I didn't really understand what I wanted until he chose me. My life was so empty before I met him. I know he's cruel, but that's only because he wants to show us what we can really be...'

Malorie put an arm round Helen and began to stroke her hair. 'You know, love, a good dom lets you find that kind of thing out for yourself,' she said, softly.

~

Ricky drove very slowly up the private road to the Master's house: there were no streetlights here and his headlamps showed him a rather dubious-looking road surface. Lance Graham, in the front passenger seat, winced slightly. 'I remember this from last night, thought the goddamn hire car was going to get stuck.'

'With the money he's got, you'd think he'd have something done about it,' Natasha grumbled. Ricky said nothing. He didn't, in all honesty, care that much; all he could think of was getting Malorie out of there. The road widened out and flattened; here was obviously all there was in the way of parking spaces. To the right of the house was a sloping driveway leading to a garage, but access to the house itself was up a flight of steps. Ricky parked, and shut off the engine, but didn't immediately move to get out of the car. A sudden stab of panic went through him: what if they'd all got it wrong? What if Malorie had fallen for the Master after all? He shook himself slightly: it couldn't be. Indianna hadn't fallen for his bullshit, so Malorie would hardly have been taken in. Behind him, Indii was fidgeting, and Natasha had undone her seatbelt and was already halfway out of the car.

'Come on, Ricky,' she said, with a touch of her old commanding manner. 'Let's get Malorie home.'

'I can't wait to see his face when we tell him he's been rumbled,' Indii giggled.

The ground floor windows of the house were in darkness, but a glow of light shone from the upper ones. Late on a Sunday night, though, where would the Master be, apart from at home? They all hurried up the steps into the porch, and Ricky got hold of the knocker and pounded it on the door. Then they waited. The night was still and cold; no wind to rustle the leaves in the trees, no sound of traffic from the road that ran past the back of the house. Ricky knocked again.

~

The Master had, in fact, been almost dozing: it had been a very late night and a most energetic afternoon. The thunderous knocking startled him, and he almost fell off the sofa. With a snarl, he got to his feet: who on earth would be disturbing him this late? He left the room and headed for the stairs, pausing at the top of them as a delightful possibility occurred to him. Only ten days ago, Malorie Jackson had turned up just as unannounced, but she was not the only cunt who had been exposed to the first stages of his Method. Perhaps rumours of the previous night's party had reached someone else who might have been feeling the power of the Master, and crystalised such an intention in her head. He descended the stairs at a leisurely pace, composing his features into a suitable expression, crossed the hall and opened the door.

For a moment, he was utterly lost for words when he saw who was there. Lance Graham, despite his failure to properly comprehend and appreciate the Master's Method, was not altogether an unwelcome guest, but to have brought Ricky Smith with him? That there were two women there as well might have been pleasing, but one was the girl who had proved herself so unsatisfactory after one night, the other a self-styled dominatrix whom the Master was simply uninterested in. He gripped the edge of the door hard, and held himself in place.

'Well?' he enquired. 'Did you leave something behind, Lance?'

~

Ricky could almost admire the little bald git's sheer front. He had to know something was up, but he was still trying to be Mr Smooth, despite the fact that the four of them probably looked less friendly than the average debt collector. Though it was Lance the Master had spoken to, the American glanced at Ricky, allowing him the opportunity to take the lead. Ricky swallowed, then said,

'We've come for Malorie, where is she?'

The Master raised his head slightly, and looked down his nose at Ricky.

'She's here,' he said. 'But here is where she wants to be. I can't imagine that you taking her away against her will would be safe, sane or consensual.'

'Oh, and what you do is?' Natasha snapped. 'You're full of shit and everyone knows it.'

'Hmm,' The Master turned his dark eyes on Natasha briefly. 'Not all women are worthy of a Master's attentions. Malorie is. You are not. That is your problem.'

Ricky tried not to lose his temper with Natasha: he understood her anger entirely, but that hadn't been a very good move. The Master had scored a point now, and he wasn't moving. He might even simply slam the door on the four of them.

'Where's Malorie?' he repeated, not really knowing what else to say.

~

Though she would wonder, later, why she hadn't simply told Helen she was leaving now, Malorie had felt, at the time, that it mattered to get through to Helen. Partly it was her own jangled nervous system, the way in which the pain of her long beating had begun to transform into the warm glow of arousal, yet had not been worked on until she reached any kind of relieving orgasm, which made her carry on caressing the other girl. Helen was still wearing the dark blue corset she had chosen that morning, her breasts spilling over the top of it, her shaved sex bare to the world.

'Do you like this?' Malorie asked as she ran her fingertips lightly over Helen's nipples. 'Does it feel good, or do you want me to stop?'

Helen said nothing, but inclined her body towards Malorie's touch. So Malorie lowered her head, took Helen's right nipple between her teeth and bit down on it, gently at first and then with increasing pressure. Helen gasped, then sighed, and Malorie released her. 'Well?' she enquired. Helen said nothing and Malorie didn't move.

'Why did you stop?' Helen asked after the silence had lengthened. Malorie bit her again.

'Do you want me to stop?' Helen shook her head. The two of them were sitting side by side on the airbed, their legs stretched out in front of them. Helen's thighs parted a little, then she opened them a little further in tentative invitation.

'Do you want some more?' Malorie asked her, placing one hand high up on the other girl's thigh. Since her first night in the house, Malorie had never done anything sexual with Helen, the Master not having seemed particularly interested in insisting that the girls caress or arouse each other in his presence. And, whether it was due to the drugs the Master had given her or the low but continuous misery of missing Ricky, Malorie had not felt particularly moved to indulge her bisexual side until now. She walked her fingertips up Helen's leg, hearing the other girl's breathing quicken, but just as she was about to make the first real approach to Helen's pussy, they both heard the sound of someone knocking determinedly on the front door. Malorie straightened up, abruptly, a sudden rush of excitement running through her. Helen whimpered and actually put her arm round Malorie to pull her closer.

'Someone at the door,' Malorie said, annoyed with herself for stating the obvious. The knock came again a moment later.

'It's nothing,' Helen said. 'Nothing important. The Master will send them away, if he even bothers to answer it. He's going to come down here soon anyway.' Now she was the one pulling away, running a hand through her hair. Impatient footsteps crossed the hall, going towards the front door.

~

The moment when the Master could have slammed the door on his unwelcome visitors had passed too quickly: Malorie's former partner had crossed the threshold and so had Lance Graham, and the women were crowding in behind them. The Master told himself firmly that they had no power over him: his Method was working successfully on Malorie

Jackson, had made her entirely his and, by all the rules of the BDSM scene, they could not take her from him against her wishes. Therefore, the simplest way to rid himself of them would be to make Malorie herself tell them to leave. He took a step back, putting himself out of reach of Smith's clenching fists, and said calmly, 'She's here. She will tell you herself that this is where she wants to be. Follow me.' He turned and headed for the dungeon rooms, sure they would do as he had said. He threw open the dungeon door, remembering, a little too late, that he had told Helen to release Malorie and look after her: the dungeon was empty so they must be in the sleeping space.

'Show yourselves, cunts!' he called, aware that the situation could slip from his control but determined not to let it.

~

Being back in the Master's house was not nearly as distressing as Indii had expected it to be. She had been tempted to stand behind either Lance or Natasha when Ricky was hammering on the door, but had told herself not to be stupid: there was nothing he could do to her now. Particularly when she knew that his self-proclaimed Method depended on drugs and hypnosis, and she had been free of either for some time. However, it was not until his dark, malicious glance passed completely over her that she felt entirely safe from him, and able to follow the others through the hall she had previously crawled across on her hands and knees. She was even able to feel a certain amused appreciation of the performance he was putting on. He must know the game was about to be up, but he wasn't admitting anything.

The dungeon playroom was as she remembered it, apart from the wooden board suspended in the middle of the room. She spared a thought to wonder what it was, but then the Master called out for Malorie, and Indii took a step back when not one but two women emerged from the inner room, both naked apart from tightly-laced corsets, both bearing the marks of recent abuse. Malorie had her head held high, and Indii noted the look of passionate relief on her face, yet she said nothing. The other girl, who Indii didn't know, displayed only an uneasy surprise.

Ricky moved round, clearly aiming to get in front of the Master, but the Master put out an arm to hold him back and said, 'You are mine, cunt. Tell your friends you are mine.' There was an utter silence, and Indii wondered if she was the only one who thought that, at least on the part of her group, it was a matter of being stunned almost to reluctant admiration of the Master's audacity. She heard Ricky swallow and shift his feet, and wondered if he genuinely believed, at some level, that the Master could take any woman he wanted. Ricky said, simply, 'I don't think she is, though.'

~

Malorie, also, had a flash of amused acknowledgement of the Master's behaviour, which was coupled with a near-shameful enjoyment of the big drama of this moment. However, it was almost immediately swamped in the knowledge that Ricky was there, right in front of her, that he hadn't stopped wanting her and worrying about her, and he had come to save her... She no longer cared about making any kind of grand announcement, she just ran to Ricky and threw herself into his open arms.

'Take me home?' she half-sobbed. 'There's loads of shit recorded, get me out of here.'

'Yeah, pal, you're fucked,' she heard the American say and, safe in Ricky's tight embrace, she raised her head to see the Master's expression of baffled fury turning to horror. Now she realised that both Madame Natasha and Indianna Livingtone were there, too, and it was Natasha who stepped up next.

'He knows, she knows, we all know,' Natasha proclaimed. 'You're a fucking shithead who drugs and rapes people and uses stupid, cheap, hypnotic tricks: bollocks to your Method, it's bullshit. You think yourself lucky we're not going to strap you down and stick half a dozen dildos up your ringpiece and make you like it. Malorie never wanted to belong to you, she wanted to stitch you up and you fucking deserve it.'

'You want to get your stuff?' Ricky murmured in her ear, and Malorie shrugged slightly then nodded. 'It's all in the room down the hall, let's go.' In fact, she barely cared that she was almost naked, and would have happily abandoned her belongings if fetching them would have meant any further entanglements with the Master. As it was, though, while he was still standing there with his mouth open, Helen suddenly burst into passionate tears and flung herself down on the floor at his feet.

'It's not true, Master, it's not true, you're MY master,' she cried, and Malorie winced. She realised that, even at the very end, she had not given Helen much consideration – though she hoped that she would have insisted on bringing the other girl away with them if Helen had asked. None of the others appeared to know what to do, so she pulled herself slightly away from Ricky and said again, 'Down the hall, let me get some clothes on and let's get out of here.'

The Master stood frozen, ignoring both their departure and Helen's sobbing pledges of devotion. The little group moved hurriedly out of the dungeon and into the hall, and Ricky tossed his car keys to the American.

'Go and get in. Natasha, Indianna, you go too, let's get out of here.' Malorie took little notice of whether they did as he said or not, aware only of Ricky's hand in hers as they ran across the hall, into the room where her clothes were. She spared only minutes to grab her black PVC raincoat and pull it on, bundle as many of her things as she could lay hands on into her holdall, and she was ready to go. They were out of the front door, down the steps and stumbling across the road when Ricky stopped for a moment and pulled her close to him.

'Shall I firebomb his fucking house or what?' he said. 'Or go back in there and kick the shit out of him? How bad was it?'

Malorie clung to him, feeling still sore, cold under her raincoat, sickened by what she had undergone, and yet satisfied.

'Just fucking take me home,' she said.

EPILOGUE

The small playroom was illuminated by candles, and the light of the full November moon, streaming in through the window: they hadn't bothered to draw the curtains. Ricky was strapped to the A-frame, facing outwards, naked, leather cuffs holding his wrists and ankles in place. Malorie, dressed in black patent leather thighboots, hold-up black fishnet stockings and a black rubber corset decorated with silver studs, affixed the final clothespeg to the flesh of his inner thigh. The pain was intense, but glorious, and he let out a long, shuddering breath. She straightened up and began to pace slowly around him, licking her lips. He writhed, feeling the hard wood of the frame hurtful against the welts on his arse and shoulders: she had previously had him bent over the little whipping stool for a serious flogging, his cock trapped in a silver-plated cockring that meant he couldn't come without her permission. She'd removed the ring a few moments after laying on the final lash, and he'd gone slightly soft, but when she ordered him to the A-frame and fastened the cuffs, he'd gotten hard again, hard enough to think he might shoot the minute she touched him. Again, she'd stepped back, waiting until he had himself under control.

~

It had been late on the Sunday night when they got home from the Master's house, even though Lance Grey had insisted that Ricky drop him, Indii and Natasha at the first minicab office they passed. Malorie had thought, knowing the thought was inconsequential and a bit irrelevant, that she should have allowed Lance to sit in the front passenger seat as sitting in the back would be uncomfortable for the long-legged American, but she had needed to be as close to Ricky as possible. There hadn't been much conversation, either before or after the other three got out of the car, and once Ricky had parked the Vauxhall at the back of the shop, she had begun to cry a little, unable to stop as they climbed the stone staircase to the little balcony where the back door of the flat was. She dropped her holdall on the kitchen floor and just stood there, sobbing quietly, until Ricky locked the door behind them and took her in his arms.

'It's OK girl, it's OK. You did brilliantly, I know you did. You're home now, you're safe now, come on girl, it's all right, I love you so much...' He'd half carried her to the bathroom, stripping her of her clothes on the way, dropping them in the narrow hallway. After a long hot shower and then a mug of whisky tea, they'd gone to bed and slept deeply, wrapped in each other's arms all night. In the morning, they'd fucked a couple of times, hot and hard and fast, and then Ricky had said he didn't think they'd open the shop today, so they'd stayed in bed the whole day, holding each other, fucking every now and again, with occasional forays to the kitchen for food or drinks and occasional bathroom calls.

On Tuesday evening Ricky had gone through the clothes she'd brought back, including the trashed red corset. He'd extracted the recording devices and downloaded the sound files, selected the most important sections and uploaded them to a couple of appropriate networks. Malorie had sat with him at the beginning, but listening to the Master speaking had upset her: she'd gone into the kitchen and shut the door, staying there till Ricky had finished. She knew she was being a bit silly, there was nothing the man could do to her now, she'd fucked him over completely. But she still expected it would take her a while to feel entirely herself again.

~

Malorie caressed the single-tail whip, eyeing Ricky as he writhed on the A-frame. There were clothespegs on his nipples, scrotum and inner thighs, and his cock was hugely erect. He looked at her for a moment, and smiled, and she raised the whip, prepared, and let fly, removing the first peg from his right nipple. She gave him next to no time to recover before wielding the whip again to snap off the peg from his left nipple. Two slow steps took her right up close to him: his eyes were shut, and he was biting into his bottom lip. She kissed him on the forehead and retreated again.

Hiss-crack, hiss-crack! Ricky gasped and moaned. Malorie ran the single tail through her fingers again, then lowered the whip to the floor. She had taken off the pegs she'd attached to the soft flesh of his thighs, and now only two remained. Her heart was pounding as she gazed on him, bound and suffering and yet loving it. Loving her, he would endure it, just as she endured the things he did to her. She went to him and wrapped her arms round him, pressing her body against his and starting to bite him, on his neck, shoulders and chest. His whole body was slick with sweat and he jerked in his restraints, pushing against her. She withdrew just far enough to remove the last two pegs from his scrotal sac, stroking his face with her other hand to transform the pain, kissing his mouth again, parting her lips for his questing tongue.

~

In her comfortable flat, Natasha Williams had been served an excellent dinner by Esmerelda, her maid. Admittedly, it had been an expensive pizza from a supermarket gourmet range, removed from its packaging and popped under the grill, but it had been elegantly presented and the wine perfectly chilled. Now, Natasha had left the table and logged on to SMLink. Esmeralda had placed an Irish coffee within reach and gone to wash up and clean the kitchen.

Natasha laughed out loud as someone in the Link chatroom tried to assert that the audioclips of the Master advocating the use of drugs to ensure proper submission were part of some anti-BDSM conspiracy, only to be stylishly shot down by about three different posters. There had already been several women posting to the effect that their encounters with the Master had had not only been creepy and non-consensual but quite the opposite of erotic. A few more had mentioned unpleasant after-effects from attending his talk at Kinktastic, and how long it had taken for these to wear off.

Esmerelda came back into the room and began to massage Madame Natasha's shoulders.

'Madame, is this mere slave going to be privileged to know what the flipping heck all this is about?'

Natasha raised one hand from the laptop to reach, unerringly, to the maid's satin-covered nipple and give it a tweak. 'Wouldn't you rather enjoy exquisite uncertainty? With a firm reassurance that justice has been done?' she enquired, and the massage turned into something that almost disrespectfully approached being a tickle.

~

It wasn't until the Friday that Malorie felt the urge. They'd spent the week stepping a little tentatively round each other, partly helped by the fact that all the customers who came into the shop had either not known or not wanted to admit to knowing anything about what had gone on. But, when they closed up and went upstairs to the flat on Friday evening, Malorie had been aware of a certain need. It had been burning in her, all day. She had turned to Ricky, the minute the connecting door was closed, and said, 'So, were you a good boy while I was away?' There had been a brief unease in saying it, in slipping into role, in case he didn't respond, but a great greedy, happy, needy smile had spread over his face.

'No, Miss. Not in the least.' he'd said.

And now she had freed his ankles and undone his wrist cuffs, and they were standing face to face in front of the A-frame, and he was trembling slightly.

'Go to the bedroom and lie on the bed,' she instructed him, and he turned and obeyed. Malorie followed him, one hand between her legs, stroking her throbbing, aching pussy.

'No one's going to ever take that knobend seriously again, are they?' she said as she climbed on top of Ricky and he reached for her tits.

'No, girl. You won. You did it,' he said, starting to move inside her. Malorie closed her eyes for a moment, relishing the sensation. 'It was for you, too,' she murmured. 'And I couldn't have done it without you. I love you, love me..'

'Love me, I love you,' Ricky said, then he said it again, thrusting up and pulling her to him, and she fell on top of him, kissing him.

~

Indianna had told herself that she only needed to go to the pre-club munch, that it was OK not to go on to Vicious Pinx afterwards, but she had dressed in PVC panties and bra, and seamed fishnet holdup stockings, before putting on a simple dark blue velvet dress suitable for the slightly Goth pub where the munch was held. She had expected a certain amount of the conversations to refer to the thoroughgoing expose of the Master and, also, for there to be a few defenders of his Method or, at least, people who professed to believe that he had been misrepresented. She hadn't quite bargained for how quickly she would become bored, embarrassed and irritated by the Master as a topic of conversation. It seemed like no one could talk about anything else, and the only consolation was that no one seemed to be aware, or to care, that she had gone over for him, or that she had been involved in the final showdown. She heard herself referred to, but not by name, more than once and grinned a rueful grin to herself: all those people saying they had heard of some girl being freaked out by the Master and leaving the scene – none of them had either known who she was or given a toss at the time. She began to feel a bit out of temper, and headed for the bar, thinking she'd have one more drink and then go home. At first, she thought that the stocky red-haired man finishing a pint of Guinness had strayed in from the live music venue at the back, until he grinned at her and said, 'You look as bored with that lot as I am'. Indii considered for a moment and then ventured, 'So, are you interesting?'

'I'm not a tosser,' the redhead said. 'And, if I'm wrong, you can either shoot me or walk away, but my mate Lance told me all about this wanker calling himself The Master. And how he's just got his... Made me think it was time to get back on the scene myself and show them all what it's really about.'

'So you know?' she queried, feeling a sudden quiver of excitement between her legs at the way he was looking her up and down.

'I know a thing or two,' he said lazily. 'You look like you do, as well.'

'Oh, I do...' Indianna said and allowed him to take her by the hand.

HUNTERS' MOON

He might well remember this all his life, just as Malorie had said he would. She was out there, somewhere, at least for a while: running, hiding, playing the game. The light was awesome, and he wondered why he'd never fully appreciated it before, the strange autumnal glow that mingled sunset and the full, risen, orange moon. He was hiding in the twilight, a weapon in his hand, and the woods were full of women. Ricky grinned to himself, adrenalin surging. A perfect night for a hunter, they'd said.

The other hunters were busy elsewhere, evidently. Somewhere behind him, he heard a female voice raised in a sudden scream; whether it was pain, pleasure or a combination of the two, he couldn't tell. One down, by the sound of it, but that left plenty more.

The scream was abruptly cut off, but now he could hear someone else, moving fast, heading for the clearing just in front of him. He licked his lips, enjoying the anticipation of prey – and then there she was, bursting through the undergrowth. It was one of the American's girls, the taller of the two, a leggy blonde with a lovely pair of small, firm tits. It was still light enough for him to get a really good look at them as she stopped, panting for breath. The front of her little white dress was ripped almost as far as her navel, and her long, dark-gold curls tumbled loose over her shoulders. He wondered what he would do with her first; a vision of himself throwing her down on the soft grass and plunging inside her, fucking that sweet little shaven quim of hers, danced in his head and his cock, already hard, gave an almost painful throb in his pants

She glanced behind her, then paused, gathering up her mass of golden hair in her hands, presumably to fasten it up and get it out of the way. He watched her, listening intently for any sound that might suggest that anyone else was approaching, but he couldn't detect anything in particular. With an anticipatory grin, he rose to his feet and stepped forward, taking a leisurely aim at his prey.

'Gotcha, Samaris,' he said, and she jumped.

'Mercy,' she whispered. 'Have mercy on a poor girlchild.' She even went to clutch at the torn neckline of the dress, making her eyes all wide and tragic, and then she gave a wicked little giggle.

'Maybe we could come to an arrangement?'

'I'm sure we could, girl. I'm pretty bloody sure we could,' Ricky said. This was going to be magnificent.

~

It had felt good from the beginning; the men gathered on the terrace in the late afternoon, sipping coffee, comparing notes, commenting on the weather and the venue.

'It really couldn't have been a better day for it,' Master Mike had said. 'Are you sure there's been no use of arcane powers here, young man?'

Ricky had laughed. 'Thought you were too old to believe in crap like that,' he said. 'Though it would have been a bugger in the rain, wouldn't it?'

Rain had been the biggest concern throughout the weeks of planning, but Malorie had insisted that the odds were good for no rain in late September. She'd picked the date after googling a load of stuff about the phase of the moon; nothing witchy about it, just an awareness of nature. And she'd been lucky with the weather, you had to give her that.

~

'You English and your goddamn weather,' Lance, over from the States,came and leaned on the parapet. His two gorgeous female companions were now down at the edge of the lawn with the rest of the girls, and he looked over at them, then turned back to Ricky and Mike.

'Do you ever talk about anything else? I sometimes wonder if you have to turn on the TV to check the forecast before you get your girls to take their panties off...'

Ricky laughed along with the rest, though he thought that at least some of this weather chat was a sign of nervous anticipation. After all, what they were going to do today was out of the ordinary, even for fetish scene veterans. Some people had heard of similar events, but they'd not been able to uncover anyone who'd actually taken part. A test, Brandon had said, a test run, at least. He'd implied that was why he'd allowed Malorie so much say over the organisation, but he had been gracious enough about it. Malorie and Ricky rarely dabbled in event hosting; the shop kept them busy enough, but from time to time, when a new challenge offered itself, well, why not take it up? Brandon could call it a test if he liked. What Ricky had said to Malorie, in the privacy of their own bed that night, was that Brandon himself was undergoing as much of a test as the event was. He was still fairly new to most of them, after all. Malorie had laughed.

'He's all right,' she said. 'Sound as a pound, I reckon.' Ricky, who trusted her instincts almost more than his own, had been reassured.

However, when she'd gone on to elaborate about exactly how tall, dark and handsome Brandon was, and how wealthy, of course, Ricky had decided she was being disrespectful and needed to be punished. In one swift, efficient move, he'd pinned her to the mattress and trapped both her hands in the loops of soft rope that were always hanging from the wooden bedhead, ready whenever they were needed. She'd laughed and called him a few choice names, and he'd climbed from the bed and stripped the covers right off.

'So, you think Brandon might be the best, do you?' he asked, in teasing tones. 'Just because he's rich, and good looking, and he's got a big house?'

Malorie didn't answer. She was licking her lips and pressing her thighs together, and Ricky saw her nipples were already crinkling up with excitement.

He opened a drawer in the bedside cabinet and pulled out a large, fake-ostrich feather, dyed bright red. Malorie caught sight of it and squealed.

'Oh no, you bastard! Don't you dare.' Ricky laid the feather down beside her and went to the other end of the bed, so he could grab her feet and tie them to the posts. He knew she'd kick like a wild pony if she got the chance.

'You look so hot like that,' he told her. 'All trapped and helpless. Maybe I ought to gag you as well.'

'You wouldn't,' she said. 'You know you want to hear the screams.'

She was quite right, but Ricky informed her that answering back would simply intensify the punishment. He did take a moment or two longer to look at her, admiring the supple curves of her body, the long legs, the vivid, expressive face he loved more than any other in the world. Then he picked up the feather and began the exquisite torture-by-tickling that he knew would reduce her to a writhing, squalling mess. When she was limp and beyond any attempt to resist, he'd suck and lick her clit until she came, and only then would he plunge his rigid, throbbing cock inside her.

~

It had been Master Mike's idea at the start, or rather one of Mike's fantasies; as he said, one of the few that he hadn't yet fulfilled. It had come up during one of the pub gossip sessions that some of them occasionally had after the monthly London Kinks market, and initially Malorie had thought that it was likely to remain just that: an unfulfillable fantasy. She'd said as much to her friend Dizzy a day or two later when Dizzy had dropped into Thrillers, the fetish shop Malorie and Ricky owned.

'It's not like anyone's got a big enough garden for that sort of thing, and I can't see it going down too well in the park with all the dog walkers and kids, can you? Even if they do have it of an evening, it'll be all yobs with bottles of cider hopping out of the bushes.'

Dizzy, however, had been quite taken with the idea.

'Tell you what, Malorie, have you met the lovely Brandon yet? Mr New Face on the Scene? He's actually got the big house in the country and a big bag of money to go with it. He's had me round there fitting out his dungeon, so it's definitely not all bullshit.'

Shortly after that, things had started to come together. Brandon, it turned out, had definite dreams of setting up as a club promoter and was more than happy to have his premises used for something that would be a talking point for years. It was coming up to Master Mike's 60th birthday, which was a good justification for staging a special event – and for making it reasonably exclusive, something both Ricky and Malorie had thought was crucial. Brandon hadn't cared much either way, but accepted that the first time you tried something new, it was best to try it on trusted friends. The final clincher had been hearing that Lance Graham, one of the biggest names on the American fetish scene, was planning his annual visit around the time they were planning to do the thing.

~

And now the day had come, and the Great Sub Hunt was under way. All the subs were female on this occasion, and they had been given a twenty-minute head start before the seven men began the pursuit. What rules there were had been kept simple but open to interpretation; there was a competitive element, there would be prizes, but the prizes had been left unspecified. The men had the weaponry, naturally, but the girls would gain points for ingenuity...

~

Indianna wasn't expecting to win anything; she considered herself only there as a spare warm body. She'd felt particularly surplus to requirements when the girls lined up at the start of the day and she saw what the others had chosen – or been instructed - to wear and compared it with what Karl, her top for the day, had insisted on dressing her in.

Lance's girls, Samaris and Nina, were in short, flirty, white dresses – OK, it was one of his trademarks to have any girls he travelled with, or was accompanied by, dressed very much the same, so she supposed it wasn't surprising. Though of course, Lance being the sort of man he was, both the American girls wore little white trainers and ankle socks as opposed to the kind of fanciful, high-heeled, many-strapped footwear they would usually be expected to wear for a fetish event. Another acquaintance of hers, Polly, was wearing a black corset which left both her breasts and her pussy bared, along with a black collar and matching cuffs, and flat black boots; there were two girls she didn't know in full latex catsuits of a brilliant pink, complete with hoods and rubber ponytails, and another, who'd been introduced to her as Donna, naked except for scarlet rubber panties and a red ball gag.

Karl had told her he would provide her costume for the day, and she had wondered if it was some kind of joke when she opened the bag he had given her and discovered leggings and a t-shirt. Putting them on had made her feel a little better, particularly as she had been ordered to go without any underwear at all. The t-shirt, in an unassuming shade of grey-green, clung snugly to her breasts yet somehow supported them, and the greeny-brown leggings were tight enough to make her understand the instruction he'd given her to shave her quim completely smooth.

Still, looking at the others had made her envious and annoyed, until she set eyes on Malorie, who was similarly attired in black and charcoal grey, with a loose grey overshirt of fine fishnet, and thigh-high but low-heeled black suede boots. Malorie had winked at her, and Karl, before sending her to join the rest, had whispered in her ear, 'You have advantages, little one. I trust you to use them. Ingenuity? You have it in abundance.'

She still wasn't quite sure what he meant. Petite, with light brown, fluffy hair and tits that were average rather than spectacular, Indii tended to fade into the background. She and Karl had engaged in several entertaining BDSM sessions, but there was nothing major between them, which she thought was one of the reasons he'd brought her along today.

~

Now she was beginning to understand what he meant. Malorie had vanished completely, within moments of Brandon's firing the starter gun – a little piece of drama which had made the rubber-suited girls clutch at each other and shriek. They, and Polly, would have been incredibly easy to find even in the fading daylight, as would the Americans. Indianna, on the other hand, was able to slink among the trees and watch what was transpiring. Miss Rubber Panties had run past her a couple of times, with additional marks on both bumcheeks and boobs on each occasion. She'd also seen Polly and Nina get trapped and shot: the guns fired different shades of gel pellets that left a definite mark and made it clear who'd hit the target. She wasn't sure what the gel would do to body-covering latex, but had decided not to worry about that. She had a few ideas, now, and was just awaiting an opportunity to put them into practice. Ingenuity, they'd said. She'd give them a dose of it, all right.

It came sooner than she expected. She spotted Ricky from some distance; his fair hair visible even though he was crouched at the base of a tree. He wasn't looking in her direction, being mostly intent on the clearing ahead of him, but as she began to sneak towards him, a commotion began, further away, which clearly distracted him. She thought it was Polly she could hear, screaming at full pitch of her lungs, but it didn't matter that much. Ricky was thinking about the noise from that direction, and unaware of any sound Indianna might make. He was still holding on to his gun, and she didn't think she was fast enough to rush up and snatch it, but there might be something she could do. Before she could formulate a proper plan, though, Samaris ran into view, and Ricky broke cover to deal with her.

It was rapidly clear how this little scene was going to play out, and Indianna, whose voyeuristic tendencies had often been encouraged by Karl, settled down to watch appreciatively as the luscious American girl dropped to her knees and began unfastening Ricky's trousers.

~

Ricky knew, on one level, that there was some risk attached to allowing himself to forget about whoever else might be stalking prey in the woods, but the opportunity was too delicious to turn down. For this particular event, it had been agreed and understood by all the invited guests that the sub girls could use their own discretion and preferences about whether or not any direct sexual contact would occur and, as Samaris had been the one to make the initial suggestion, Ricky was going to take full advantage of her offer. She looked bloody gorgeous, kneeling on the rough grass at his feet, all tousled and half-undressed. He could see enough of her tits to be aware that her nipples were erect, and when she raised her face to look at him, her eyes were full of a wicked excitement, her pupils dilated.

'I'm good, sir,' she murmured. 'Wait till you see how good I can be.'

'Better be the truth, hadn't it?' he remembered to say. 'Or else...'

She'd been skilfull about unfastening his black combat pants just enough to allow her access to his cock, which had been almost fully hard for the past half hour. Now, as her supple, clever fingers stroked the length of it, it stiffened some more, and he was aware of how full and heavy his balls had become. He arched his back and, almost unthinkingly, let the gun fall from his hand as Samaris opened her mouth and took the whole length of his rod inside. It was a while since anyone other than Malorie had sucked him off, and though she had a variety of techniques, it still felt noticeably different to have the lovely blonde use her lips and tongue on him. Samaris favoured a hard, greedy sucking, her lips tightening and relaxing on the base of his shaft in a steady rhythm, one hand lightly cupping his balls while the other rested on his buttocks, keeping his whole lower body still and focussed on the sensations she was giving him. He was dimly aware of a degree of vulnerability here, standing in the middle of the woods with his dick in a woman's mouth, not exactly prepared if anyone should come along and intervene, but it didn't really matter. Nothing mattered but that powerful, steady suction, which was increasing in intensity, and he was going to lose it any minute and shoot his load, and he really couldn't last very much longer, and he thought he ought to say something to her, give her at least a little bit of warning, but she'd moved her hand in order to apply a little bit of pressure on that holy, hypersensitive space between his balls and his arsehole, and now his hips were jerking frenziedly and he was shouting out, some unfocussed senseless noise, and coming, coming, coming...

~

It had been hard not to giggle with anticipation as she crawled on her belly across the clearing. Indianna had to bite her lips quite hard as she got within reach of the gel gun Ricky had dropped. She thought for a moment that Samaris had spotted her and tipped her an encouraging wink, but it was equally possible that the other girl's eyes had closed as she was transported by her own passionate concentration. She had just made it back to the cover of the trees when Ricky pulled out and took a step back. Samaris licked her lips and smiled.

'You goin' to let me run along, now?' she asked. Ricky appeared to be considering it.

~

'He should, because I've got a gun on you both. Run along, blondie!'

While Samaris, with a shriek of laughter, got to her feet and ran back the way she had come, Ricky looked around in a clear whirl of confusion and annoyance. Indianna froze where she was, aware that the voice had come from very, very close behind her. Maybe whoever it was wouldn't see her if she kept really, really still. The moment seemed to stretch out endlessly; long enough for Indianna to wonder which option she preferred – to be ignored, and free to score some points, or to be seized and punished. There was a quivering tension in both her quim and her bumcheeks, and she tried to hold her breath, but failed. All of a sudden, her ingenuity seemed to have vanished.

'Relax, mate, I've got another fine bird we can play with. Right... here!' A hand closed on the back of Indianna's t-shirt and gave a leisurely pull. Rather than let it rip, she scrambled up, but made no attempt to escape. Ricky was grinning at her across the clearing, and Indianna relaxed; he was someone she'd known for a good few years, and thoroughly trusted even though they had rarely played together. Her captor, on the other hand... She turned her head to glance back at him, and gave a little shiver of nervy excitement. She'd never actually met Brandon before this event, and she wasn't sure she'd heard anything at all about his particular perversions. He was a big man, at least six feet tall and solid.

Just as she was reminding herself of this, Brandon picked her up with one hand and slung her over his shoulder in one smooth movement, and Indianna squeaked in surprise.

'What are you going to do with her?' Ricky sounded slightly put out.

'Don't worry, I'm happy to share. There's just a better spot to take her, back over this way. Come on, I want to do her before the light goes completely.'

'Fair point. Must be getting close to the end of it now,' Ricky agreed and, though she couldn't really see him from her upside-down position, Indianna could tell he was following as Brandon carried her away. Nothing quite like this had ever happened to her before, but it was definitely exciting. He had one arm locked firmly round her waist, trapping her arms by her sides. It didn't seem to have occurred to him that she might wriggle or kick. As soon as it occurred to her, though, she decided not to start. For one thing, she didn't fancy being dropped from shoulder height, which might happen accidentally if she kicked him somewhere sensitive. Also, she was enjoying the experience of feeling utterly overpowered.

A few minutes later, they had reached the path that led through the centre of the woods and were almost back to the lawn: Indianna knew this was so because there was light coming from a row of big, free-standing lanterns, each filled with a thick church-style candle, which someone must have lit as the last of the light began to fade. Brandon set her down on her feet and took a firm grip on her hair.

'Anything you particularly fancy doing to her, Ricky? I'll let you go first.'

~

Ricky was intrigued to see Brandon in action. He and Malorie had got to know the man a little in the course of planning the event, as well as running into him from time to time in clubs, but he couldn't recall ever seeing him do anything to anyone. He'd wondered if Brandon, as host of the hunt, would sustain his general detachment on the grounds of being the one in charge, and was keen to know what would happen next.

Having come explosively in Samaris' mouth only a little while ago, he didn't plan on screwing Indianna, cute though she was. Also, he could feel himself sliding more into the role of sidekick and junior participant in this upcoming scene.

'We could see if she's taken any hits so far,' he suggested, and then glanced back down the path.

'Mind you, I think a few of the others might be back up here any minute, so we might have witnesses.'

'Witnesses are fine by me,' Brandon said, with a grin some people might have called satanic. 'The more the merrier. In fact, I can see some now.'

With his free hand, he pulled a pair of cuffs from his pocket and tossed them to Ricky, who only just managed to catch them.

'Cuff her to the fence, there. And get her pants down.'

He let go of Indianna's hair, and Ricky wondered if she might run away, but she stood there, entirely submissive and, when Ricky took her arm, he saw that her expression was eager, her eyes wide and her lips moist. It made his cock stir again, and he grinned at her.

'Come on,' he told her. 'Don't keep us waiting.'

She went with him willingly, and bent over without being asked, gripping the upper rail of the wooden fence. She stayed in position as he snapped the cuffs in place, looping the chain between them around the rail so she couldn't change her mind and make a run for it. Remembering that Brandon had instructed him to bare the girl's bottom, he tugged down her leggings to below the knee, immobilising her further. She was nude underneath them, and quite unmarked.

'No hits at all!' he reported, straightening up.

'I thought there wouldn't be,' came another voice, and Ricky realised that several of the other guests had joined them. Lance, with an arm round each of his girls, both of whom were in some disarray but grinning mischievously, as was the American; Master Mike, gripping Polly by the ring in her collar, and

Karl, the sardonic, stocky dom who had brought Indianna along to the hunt. He was the one who had spoken, and he went on now.

'That's just the sort of bad girl she is; hiding in the bushes, cheating...' He was smiling as he said it, and a look passed between him and Lance, who was the person who probably knew Indianna the best out of all of them. 'Feel free to punish her.'

'Oh, I will,' Brandon said. He raised his voice a little, glancing round at them all; Ricky noticed that Malorie had quietly emerged from the trees and was watching intently.

'I'm going to beat her and then I'm going to fuck her. Ricky, do you want to warm that lovely arse of hers up for me?'

Malorie was nodding in appreciation and Ricky got it: for all the grandstanding, Brandon was reading everyone's cues, giving anyone who needed it the opportunity to deflect him, making sure that no one, especially Indianna, had any objections. It was masterfully done, in every sense and everyone clearly got it.

~

Ricky positioned himself behind the handcuffed girl and ran his hands over the peachy curves of her arse. Her skin was slightly cool to the touch, and he didn't want to draw the process out too long.

He began to spank her, lightly at first but quickly increasing the intensity, building up the rhythm, left cheek then right cheek then back again, pausing from time to time to stroke and gently rub, feeling the glowing warmth of the flesh as it responded. Her breathing was getting a little ragged and she had begun to whimper when he took a step back and raised his eyebrows at Brandon.

The bigger man slowly unfastened his wide leather belt and drew it out of the loops on his black leather trousers.

'She ready for me?'

Ricky nodded, moving further away as Brandon took up a position, the belt doubled over in his left hand.

~

It landed with a fine, sharp crack and Indianna yelped. Bottom warmed to perfection by the hand-spanking, she still found the first one a jolt to her whole system. It was followed by another, then another, and she felt the bite of each one, harsh for a moment and then somehow shifting into a delicious spreading heat. It wasn't just her rear that was sizzling, though; her pussy had been feeling steadily more slippery-hot with every minute of anticipation as Ricky cuffed her to the fence and stripped her. She was aware, though only vaguely, that quite a few people were watching her take this punishment and though she'd done, and submitted to, various things in clubs and at parties, it had never been as thrilling as this; in the woods, near dark now, cuffed to a fence, with the man behind her an unknown quantity, tall, dark, powerful and single-mindedly beating her. She gave another sharp cry and realised that she was almost on the verge of orgasm.

He paused; she heard him step back, and it was very hard not to protest; she could take more, she was nowhere near at the end of her endurance. Then he was up close behind her, his hands moving firmly but gently over her bumcheeks and down, down between them, his fingers probing her juicy slit. He made a small sound of satisfaction, and then came the distinctive noise of a zip being opened. Indianna found her voice again and whimpered, 'Please.'

'What's that? Speak!'

'Please. Fuck me. Yes, do it, please…'

And then he was inside her, plunging straight in, and his cock was big, big as she might have expected, bigger than Karl's, and rock hard, and he knew how to use it. She dug her nails into the fence, groaning with pleasure, rocking her hips back against him, wanting him deeper and deeper and, oh god, she was going to come, he was going to make her come in front of Karl and Lance and everyone and it felt amazing. He obviously felt her lose control; he grabbed her hips and held her steady, driving deep inside and riding out the spasms of her quim as she howled and roared. She'd never made a noise like that in public but she didn't care.

He pulled out at the last second, squirting a couple of scalding jets of spunk across her arsecheeks, and her legs were too wobbly to hold her so she sank down to her knees, and then Ricky was uncuffing her hands and giving her a friendly pat on the shoulder before Brandon gathered her up and hugged her, his body powerful and warm as she leaned into his massive strength.

'Good girl,' he murmured, and kissed her lightly on the forehead. Still holding her, he turned to the gathered crowd, transforming himself smoothly into the host again.

'OK, back to the house. Change if you need to, dinner in about twenty minutes.'

~

Malorie, now in her favourite midnight-blue latex minidress, took another sip of wine and sighed with quiet satisfaction. Her own camouflage outfit had been agreed with Brandon, Ricky and Master Mike beforehand, and the purpose of it was not so much to gain advantage in the game, but to allow her to slip away halfway through and attend to the food. Not that it was more than a matter of laying out the platters of smoked fish, cold cuts, bread, cheese and salad but still, someone had to do it and it had been thought inappropriate, just this once, to call in the usual handful of TV maids who were so useful at Master Mike's parties.

She looked down the table at Ricky, who was sitting between Samaris and Caroline, one of the girls who'd been dressed in a latex catsuit for the hunt and who had shed it in favour of a shocking-pink satin corset and long pink net skirt. She and her fellow catsuit-wearer, Honey, had been awarded gift sets of massage oils as their prizes for having been shot most often; as the gel-and-paint combination fired by the guns tended to slide off the smooth rubber, the men had kept on shooting at the two of them in an effort to make their marks, and once they had shown off the startling array of small bruises peppering their bodies, Mike and Brandon had agreed that they deserved to win. Samaris, having been shamelessly grassed up for bribery and corruption by Ricky, had won the promise of six strokes of the cane from Lance, who had been awarded a bottle of champagne for most shots on target, as far as anyone could reliably tell from the paint stains on Polly, little Donna of the nothing-but-red-panties outfit and Samaris herself.

Ricky, apparently, hadn't managed to shoot anyone, but Malorie knew he'd had plenty of fun all the same. She caught his eye and raised her glass; he picked up a nearby bottle of red and came over to join her.

'Good time had by all, then?' he murmured, pouring her more wine.

'You bet. Especially Indianna.'

They both paused to watch the dainty brunette who was kneeling on the floor between Brandon and Karl, who were engaged in a lively conversation above her head.

'What do you think's going to happen there?' Ricky asked. Malorie said she didn't know. As it was, she had a few other things in mind, such as persuading Brandon to host another hunt in the spring. Only this time it would be the femdoms' turn to hunt a whole pack of male slaves through the spring undergrowth. Malorie took another drink. That was the best of being a switch, you got to try everything at least twice.

THE LUCKY 13TH

The mannequin in Thrillers' window was wearing a scarlet sequinned corset, with black sequinned hearts on the cups, and a black g-string, which was also heart-shaped. In its silver hand was a red silk rose, and its blank, silver face was marked with red lipstick kisses.

'That would look great on you,' Indianna observed. 'For Chained Heat, next week, the Valentine ball, obviously, but you could wear it again.'

Cerise looked at the display. Indianna wasn't wrong: despite being displayed on a standard slender mannequin, the corset was obviously the type that would look its best on a woman with curves and cleavage, like Cerise.

'I don't know,' she said, though she coveted the corset. 'I mean, I'll be in the DJ box most of the night anyway, so I wasn't going to make a big deal out of it.'

Indianna turned round and stared at her, raising her eyebrows in an exaggerated manner. 'What kind of a pervert are you anyway?' she asked in mock-shock tones.

'A skint one,' Cerise laughed, hoping it didn't sound too forced. Though she knew her friend wasn't seriously probing her motivations, she had lately been wondering about that herself. Relatively new to the whole fetish scene, she was still a little unsure of where she stood and what she wanted from it. Sure, she'd always been open-minded or so she liked to think, and she'd gained the general impression that anything consensual was OK with these new-found friends, but still... There had been some action; she'd had some fun, and a fair few orgasms, without wanting or needing anything deeper than casual playtimes. She wasn't even sure that she wanted a relationship in this case, or if one was even possible. She'd tried to tell herself she was having a crush, that was all it was; that it probably wasn't reciprocated. Though she'd often enjoyed the feverish speculation that characterized those days when you'd met someone, and there had been that feeling of intense communication, of something special about to happen, she hadn't said anything to anyone since it all began. She just couldn't find the words.

She supposed a lot of it was not wanting to look like an ignorant newbie: there had been a degree of condescension in the way some people had treated her on her first few DJ bookings that had grated but, now she was making friends, she was less bothered by it. It was just – well, it was the old thing of not wanting to make herself look stupid. That, and a fear of being thought rude as well as ignorant, and maybe giving offence to the last person in the world she'd want to offend.

She tried to derail the train of her thoughts as Indianna made for the shop's entrance, telling her to come on, at least they could have a look, see what else was on offer, but her mind kept sliding back to last Friday's gig at Fetishworld. She'd been enjoying herself: a few requests for tracks, a few compliments on her choices, the awareness that she was doing bloody well tonight when it came to keeping her mind off a certain person, who she was not, she kept telling herself, looking out for. There was no need to fill a dancefloor here and, indeed, the more esoteric the tracks, the more the majority of the punters seemed to like it. So, in the last few minutes of the set, without really thinking, or at least without admitting to herself she was thinking about it so much, she'd put on this old album track from the 70s. She had it with her, it fitted nicely with the song she'd just played, and she just wanted to hear it again. Does Everyone Stare? by The Police, a curious, fractured, haunting three minute hymn to obsession, and she could have ridden it out with a wry smile, but then she glanced up, part way through hunting out what she was going to play next, and their eyes met for a moment.

It had only been a moment: the room was crowded, and everyone had things to do, she was sure. But it had set her off again, thinking crazily about how it would be, lips on lips, those strong, capable hands touching her body, stroking her and then pulling her closer with mounting passion and then... what would happen next? That was the question, of course. The strange crashing, pulsing piano chords of the song seemed to vibrate through her whole body, and her nipples went tight and taut as she dropped her gaze, feeling herself blush, heat suffusing her. She'd managed to stick the next track on and the next one, but when Big Phil jumped up into the booth to take over, she'd barely managed to be polite to him before rushing off to the Ladies and locking herself in the end cubicle. She'd leaned her forehead against the cool melamine wall for a few minutes, breathing hard, wondering if she dared go out there and go looking, say something, ask, offer, or even beg, and then she'd unzipped her PVC jeans and thrust her hand between her legs, thinking: come and find me now, kiss me hard, kiss me and do me, I saw you looking at my mouth and then you looked away, it's not just me that's thinking like this, is it? And in all this incoherence her middle finger had found her clit and was rubbing, rubbing, the little bead of flesh firm and slick with desire, her vulva aching, a dull trembling in the pit of her stomach, and she braced her spread legs and squeezed her eyes shut, and came very hard.

Dizzy normally liked hanging out in Thrillers, catching up on the gossip with whichever of the proprietors happened to be behind the counter – whether it was Ricky or Malorie's turn to be off sourcing stock, or dealing with admin or just having a lie in upstairs. Ricky was more likely to offer a cup of tea to a longstanding, thirsty and, Dizzy hoped, well-liked supplier, though Malorie usually had the best gossip and the most interesting point of view. Dizzy liked original viewpoints, as you do when you're a bit of an original yourself. Dizzy also liked the kind of advice Malorie or Ricky dished out when you had a problem. Dizzy had mainly overheard, rather than been the direct recipient of, any advice Malorie offered on sorting out a tangled love life, but had perceived the advice to be useful. It was not a thought to be admitted, that going here today had partly been inspired by a small but miserable wish to actually ask for some advice along those lines.

Of course, it hadn't happened. All very well reassuring yourself that these people are your friends, are not judgemental, are quite capable of dealing with frankly unexpected behaviour, but it's quite another thing to put your hand up and say, you know the impression I always give? Well, it's not entirely the right one. When it started out, it was part game, part political statement, and it took on a life of its own, and the other thing didn't matter. But now, all of a sudden, it does matter. It matters a lot, and what am I going to do?

Perhaps, if it had been Malorie's day in the shop rather than upstairs, Dizzy would have cracked and confessed. As it was, with Ricky leaning against the till and discoursing semi-seriously on the joys of true love, Dizzy had taken refuge in a rant about Valentine's Day.

'Just because it's on a fucking Saturday, you'd have thought at least someone, somewhere, would have realised that half the perverts in town want to escape all that romance-and-red-roses crap. Mind you, I'm amazed the venue let them book the night, after all, they could charge much more if they opened it to the normals and gave them heart-shaped stickers on every packet of fucking crisps. Fucking normals, it's no more than they deserve.'

'So, you're not going, then?' Ricky said, with a smirk that was infuriating, even though there was no malice in it. 'You're going to stay at home and watch the telly with a bottle of gin and a ready meal, are you?'

Dizzy was tempted, for a moment, to say: Yeah, I'm going to do just that. Tell them they can collect the frames and the backdrop in the afternoon, I'm not coming out on Saturday, I hate Valentine's Day. You know I hate Valentine's Day, it's nothing to do with me, or my life, is it? But I can't say that, I want to go even though I know I shouldn't. Because if she's there, and she will be there, and if I see her, I might think I might say something like, look, will you have dinner with me? And then I'll want to kiss her and if I kiss her once I'll want to snog the face off her, and, oh, this is so ludicrous. She can't think anything more about me than Eccentric Old Freak with a good line in conversation. OK, maybe the topping thing, maybe there's something there.

Dizzy couldn't think back to that particular scene without a rush of blood to the head, and maybe a few other places, as well. It had happened towards the end of the night, when the place was starting to empty of people, and maybe that had been why. That cheeky sub with the pert little arse, going, bet the two of you together wouldn't be enough for me, and Cerise saying, we'll see about that, come on, Dizzy, help me out here.

'You should go.' Ricky's statement came after a long enough pause to make Dizzy jump slightly. 'The music's going to be good, for one thing.'

Dizzy was temporarily breathless, almost panicked. Did Ricky suspect something? Did Ricky know? Oh, fuck, was it anywhere near visible? Visible enough for people to be talking about it?

Ricky had the air of someone about to say something else, a kind of compassion on his face, but then the shop door swung open and Indianna walked in and behind her – Oh, hell, this wasn't fair at all – Cerise herself. Even dressed down, she was lovely: her black hair in a loose ponytail over one shoulder, big black sheepskin coat and flat black boots, understated make-up – and there was Dizzy in uninteresting grey combats, long red-gold curls a mess, no slap at all. Cerise looked taken aback and Dizzy tried not to wince. Let me out of here, OK. That's obviously squashed flat any interest she might have had, and it's probably all to the good, now let me go.

'Hey, Cerise,' Ricky was saying. 'Got your playlist for Saturday? Going to be doing any special requests, are you?' Cerise laughed, and blushed a little. 'Maybe, if you ask me nicely.' She cleared her throat. 'Hi Dizzy, how's it going.'

'Oh, you know. Totally busy, stuff to build, people to see. Ricky I'll call you about that cage, OK?'

~

'Funny old thing,' Indianna observed, without much interest, as Dizzy made a rapid exit. Cerise swallowed hard, fighting a rush of humiliated foolishness: she must have given herself away somehow, been embarrassing. Otherwise, surely, that headlong rush out of the shop wouldn't have happened. Dizzy would have stayed, chatted, they'd all have had a laugh together and maybe she'd have said, how about a quick drink down the road and... Stop it, she told herself. She turned swiftly back to Ricky and asked, 'Anything you specially want to hear? Have you and Malorie got a favourite song?'

Ricky grinned, running a finger over his blond moustache. 'Ah, you can choose one for us. You generally play good stuff, after all.'

Cerise was gratified. She didn't know Ricky or Malorie that well, but knew they were people whose opinion mattered, and the praise sounded sincere. A combination of pleasure at this recognition and something else she wouldn't want to label made her say, 'Well, thanks. That red corset in the window, have you got it in a 14?'

~

In bed that night, Ricky and Malorie were talking over the day's events. Malorie had been having lunch with a couple of magazine distributors, who wanted Thrillers to stock their range of fetish-themed titles. Malorie never turned down a free meal, but had no inclination to take the magazines, which were lowest-common-denominator housewives-in-rubber tat. Now she was grumbling mildly about the unreconstructed attitudes of some people who wanted to sell to the BDSM scene without understanding it.

'Honestly, silly sods, it's like they still think that only men are interested in smut. I did ask them if they'd ever thought of doing a mag aimed at women and they looked at me like I was losing the plot completely. Not that I want them to, it would just be a load of gay mag stock shots and vibrator adverts, they couldn't think beyond that if they tried.'

'Speaking of men,' Ricky began, and Malorie put her hand on his cock.

'Yes, love, I know what men are.'

'Well,' Ricky was undeterred. 'Dizzy came by. We were just having a chat and then believe it or not, Indianna showed up with Cerise the DJ, right then, just like that.'

'Ooh! So, what happened?' Malorie demanded, beginning to stroke him gently, trailing the pads of her fingers up and down his length and over and around his balls. Ricky groaned.

'It was funny. Mm, not funny exactly. Dizzy kind of flounced out in a hurry, wouldn't look at her. She bought one of the red heart corsets, though. Looked brilliant in it. I don't know if you're right or not, but there's definitely something going on with Dizzy at the moment. Whether it's anything to do with Cerise, though. I mean, has she got a partner? Mmm, that's nice, don't stop.'

He had his arm round her and now he moved his hand onto her breast and started playing with the nipple, which erected under his touch.

Malorie commenced a long, slow, languid pulling movement, her hand gripping the base of his shaft, sliding almost off the head, then loosening her grip to slither back down and start again.

'Go on,' she said. 'Do you think they're at it, and not wanting anyone to know?'

Ricky exhaled with pleasure and closed his eyes. 'Nah.' He rolled onto his side and ran his other hand over the curve of her bum, then round between her buttocks, as she slipped her leg between his, still keeping hold of his cock, and began to rub the tender head of it against her clit, using it to pleasure herself. Ricky kissed her, mouth hard against her mouth, parting her lips with his tongue, and she lay back, drawing him on top of her, guiding his hot sex inside her and bringing her hands up to rake her nails lightly and repeatedly down his spine, and dig them gently into his arsecheeks.

Though much of their sex life together involved a lively variety of whippings, spankings, bondage and roleplay, there were times when neither of them wanted anything more elaborate than this; what Malorie sometimes called a midweek fuck: short and sweet and simple. He got his fingers into position to tease and caress her clit, his hand squeezed between their bodies, getting sticky-slippery with her juices, and then she was coming, shuddering against him, and her warm, slick cunt engulfing his rod so he started to move faster, faster, listening to her gratified moans, feeling her teeth gently nip his earlobe as he reached his own peak of excitement.

It was only afterwards, when they were holding each other quietly, their muscles relaxing, that Malorie reverted to the conversation they'd been having.

'Have you ever noticed the way we all talk about Dizzy, though?' she asked, quite suddenly and Ricky frowned.' Everyone likes Dizz, though, don't they?' he said.

'That's not what I mean. Look, how many people say,' she paused then went on, 'he's -'

'Hang on, she -' Ricky stopped. 'No, hang on. Look, I've never asked, I wouldn't want to - ' He stopped again.

'People really try to avoid it, don't they?' Malorie was musing. 'Have you ever heard anyone say, he, she, him, her about Dizz without looking a bit, you know, looking over their shoulders to see if anyone's heard them say the wrong thing?'

'Heard people arguing about it,' Ricky said. 'Usually about what's polite, you know, she when she's in drag or whatever, he when he's not. But then half the time, what's drag and what ain't? I've never seen Dizzy in a frock, not ever. But there's the make up, and the heels and stuff. I heard someone say she was a butch dyke with a glam streak.'

'And then someone else probably piled in with some transgender rights stuff', Malorie observed.

'But, you know, I don't actually know what Dizzy is. I mean, I really don't know, and I don't know anyone who does. Dizz is just Dizz and always has been.'

Ricky suddenly snickered. 'Remember when that silly cow Angela actually asked? And Dizz said, well as you're never going to get to have sex with me, I don't see what the fuck it's got to do with you.'

'What do you think Cerise thinks?' said Malorie. 'I mean, I've seen Cerise with men, I reckon she's basically straight, but then again. Do you think she thinks Dizzy's a bloke? Do you think Dizzy is a bloke?'

'I've never seen Dizz with anyone,' Ricky remarked. 'Not ever. That's what threw me when you said they might be shagging. You know, Cerise.'

'I don't think they are.' Malorie snuggled closer to him. 'They want to, though. I told you about those looks, the way they look at each other. But I don't think either of them knows what to do with each other. I think that might be a problem.'

'You might be right, love,' Ricky said with a yawn. 'But it probably isn't actually our problem.'

~

Cerise hadn't planned to go to the Friday 13th munch the night before the Ball. However, Pat from Chained Heat had rung her at work that afternoon and asked if she could possibly take a batch of Ball flyers down to the Swan and scatter them around the tables as the whole Chained Heat team were embroiled in the finishing touches and all that: Cerise had said yes, of course, and thanked her lucky stars that even when absorbed in the straightworld, doing yet another temping job, she was reasonably well turned out, sharply-cut black skirt, heels, a scarlet knitted top that wasn't low-cut but still clung nicely. If she went straight from work to Pat's, picked up the flyers and then on to the Swan, she'd look OK, still. And there would be others worse dressed, of course, as if that mattered. As she hurried up the street ahead of the icy wind, making for the warmly-lit Swan, she finally allowed herself to speculate on the likelihood of Dizzy being there, before telling herself that the idea was ludicrous. For one thing, Dizzy and Cerise had initially bonded over a mutual disdain for munches, for another, Dizzy, the perfectionist, would surely be spending this evening in the workshop, fiddling with all the props and artwork and stuff that were needed for the Ball.

The munch was, as she had anticipated, not that exciting. People were mainly talking about either Valentine's Day and whether or not they had Ball tickets, or ranting about how much bad luck they'd had all day and that there must be something in it, this Friday 13th business. Cerise distributed her flyers, and agreed, cheerfully, to consider various musical requests for the following night, in between sneaking glances at her watch and wondering how long before she could reasonably make a move.

Just after nine o'clock, she spotted Leon, owner of one of the better gossip and information websites, brandishing a BlackBerry decorated with silver star stickers, which looked oddly familiar. Leon noticed her glance and turned to her immediately. 'Course – you're crew for tomorrow, you'll be in early. Can you give this to that daft tart Dizzy? We were doing an interview this morning round at mine, and then this afternoon I realised that this was still sitting on my kitchen bloody table. So, of course, there's no way of phoning up and saying,' Oi, you left your Blackberry, is there? Can't even send an email.'

Cerise took the device and almost dropped it, biting her lip in sudden rage at her own idiocy. It's a glorified mobile fucking phone, that's all, that just happens to belong to someone I fancy the arse off, get a grip. She meant to say something brightly non-committal but obliging, but what actually came out of her mouth was, 'The workshop's on my way home, I'll drop it round. Poor Dizz must be going frantic for it.'

~

Elbows on knees, chin in hands, Dizzy was sitting hunched up on the bench at the end of the workshop, feeling stupid, cross and thoroughly fed up. All very well to mutter about the ubiquity and annoyingness of modern communication gadgetry and how much you'd like to do without it, until you do something bright like lose your BlackBerry and have no idea how to get in touch with anyone to track down its whereabouts. Friday the fucking 13th, all right. And tomorrow would be Valentine's Day, with the Valentine's Ball, full of people either flaunting their couplehood or desperately trying to jump on the couple bandwagon. Dizzy snarled, then sighed, wondering what Cerise thought about the trappings of traditional romance. Roses are red, violets are blue, I'm nuts about you, but what can I do?

The sudden banging on the workshop door was an almighty shock, and Dizzy jumped up, reflexively, catching a good crack on the elbow from a half-finished A-frame in the process.

'Oh, for fuck's sake!' A quick scoot across the floor to the front, a wrestle with the bolt, which was as recalcitrant as ever, and oh what the hell else was this day going to throw up? Because there was Cerise, wide-eyed and slightly windblown, big coat framing her body in still-sexy work clothes, and looking, well, gorgeous as ever, but seriously on edge.

'What are you doing here?' Dizzy barked, regretting it the minute the words were out. Cerise recoiled, as well she might, then tightened her lips.

'You left this at Leon's' she said, producing the Blackberry from her coat pocket. 'I said I'd drop it round to you.' But I wonder why I bothered, was the unspoken conclusion.

'Oh. Oh, right.' Dizzy didn't entirely know what to think. When you don't know what to say, sometimes it doesn't hurt to say nothing, of course, because in that moment of silence, Cerise had stepped through the rickety wooden door and was standing inside the workshop, looking around her and nibbling her lower lip.

'Look, Dizzy...' She seemed to gather her resources. 'I, um, I wanted to say, after the other week, I think, maybe I - '

'Right.' Here it would come then, the 'I only think of you as a friend, and anyway aren't you...' speech. Dizzy felt a stab of regret for the friendship they'd been building up, the meeting of two minds on the same wavelength, and the way such a thing never did survive the acknowledgement that one of the friends wanted more. Oh, say your piece and go, Cerise, darling girl, I'll cope, it doesn't matter, and no one will ever know if I spend the rest of the night sitting on the floor in here crying my eyes out.

~

It had only been in the last few seconds before knocking that Cerise had come to the decision that she was going to say something, at any rate try to get some idea of how much of a fool she might be making of herself. Someone must have spotted something, or said something, and now Dizz was horribly embarrassed about it, and Cerise had to reassure her friend that it was OK, she wasn't going to make a bunny-boiling pest of herself.

But somehow, the words just wouldn't come, and Cerise looked up for a moment, and spotted something like agony in the amber eyes gazing down at hers.

'Cerise, don't stress, please,' Dizzy was saying. 'I'll get over it, OK? You're gorgeous and funny and smart and maybe you shouldn't be surprised when people fall for you, but I promise I won't ever hassle you about it.'

'Whu?' Cerise managed, inelegantly, and then she stopped. Dizzy stood still in front of her, face tense, body even more so, saying nothing more.

And then it all seemed so utterly simple that Cerise almost laughed.

'What a pair of prats we are,' she said. She reached up with both hands, pulled Dizzy's head down to hers and pressed one firm kiss on the full lips, which immediately opened, and Dizzy's arms were suddenly round her, pulling her close. They kissed on, and now they were backed up against one of the pillars in the workshop, grinding against each other. Dizzy's hands were under her coat, inside it, running up and down her back and over the curve of her arse cheeks, squeezing and caressing. Cerise in turn was stroking her friend's hair, running her fingers through the long messy red curls and tracing the line of Dizzy's cheekbone and jaw. She spread her legs a little to improve her balance, and Dizzy held her tighter. The length of Dizzy's body was moulded to hers, all hard muscles and strength and sheer heat, detectable even through two sets of clothes. Cerise's nipples were up in taut points and she moaned aloud when Dizzy lifted a hand to them, cupping her tits and squeezing gently. Now her quim was opening up, juicing up, as their legs intertwined, and she could feel that firm powerful thigh between her own pressing right on her pleasure centre.

There was a pile of dustsheets on the floor, less than a foot away, and Cerise glanced at them and decided they would do. She backed away from the embrace and shrugged out of her coat, tossing it aside. She couldn't speak, couldn't think of anything to say; she just lay down on the jumble of fabric and held out her arms. For one brief moment, Dizzy looked uneasy, then gave a shrug and knelt beside her, bending to kiss her again. Cerise pulled up her skirt and slid her own hand into her panties, cupping her mound, feeling the heat and the wetness of it, and then Dizzy's hands were there as well, tugging down tights and panties, baring her, and Cerise spread her legs as wide as she could, hearing and feeling the faint rip of nylon as the crotch of the tights split apart.

'Beautiful,' Dizzy whispered. 'You're so beautiful.' Powerful fingers twined in Cerise's damp pubic curls, and then began to explore the folds of her slippery cunt. She moaned, pushing her hips forward and Dizzy fingered her clit, circling it, applying a gentle but insistent pressure. One finger eased inside her, then another, and Dizzy was leaning over her, body angling down closer, and Dizzy's tongue was on her hot spot, tasting her, hot and wet and teasing, and Cerise cried out, something frantic and incoherent and the licking and the fingerfucking speeded up. It was almost unbearably delicious. Cerise moaned and clutched at the sheets, rolling her head from side to side, aware that orgasm was imminent, feeling the little quiverings in her stomach and the muscles of her thighs, a sense of pressure building in her quim. She bore down, gripping Dizzy's plunging fingers with her pussy walls, and then the moment was on her, inescapable and immense, a long, screaming convulsion of delight.

'Holy fucking shit,' Dizzy murmured. 'It's about five years since I did anything like that.'

Cerise reached out, wanting more contact, another embrace, needing the closeness. They hugged, stroking one another's hair, pressing their bodies together.

'I want –' Cerise stopped, and they gazed at one another. She took a deep breath and tried again.

'Tell me what to do for you,' she whispered. 'Just tell me. That was just the beginning, wasn't it? I don't want to stop.'

Dizzy's head dropped on her shoulder for a moment, and the words were faint but still audible.

'Nor do I, but... Cerise do you know? I mean, do you mind? I haven't... I haven't done anything for years.'

'That's OK,' Cerise suddenly laughed. 'I'll be gentle with you, love.'

The perfect thing to say popped into her mind. 'You can even keep your pants on. Or not.'

Dizzy sat up then, looking stunned, but delighted.

'I really don't care,' Cerise said, as firmly as she dared. 'Dizzy, honestly, I don't.'

'Well, let's at least get upstairs, then,' Dizzy said.

The kiss was a little clumsy, but heartfelt on both sides. The rest of the night was going to be interesting.

HANDS-ON RESEARCH

Cerise had a feeling that, at some point fairly soon, Indianna was going to ask her The Question. All she could really do, she supposed, was try to spot it coming and deflect the conversation; she didn't want to have a row or be accused of... well, what? Wanting a little privacy? Being overly defensive? Being ashamed of her choices? She wasn't in the least ashamed, but nor did she want to have the source of her happiness picked over by other people who didn't know the things she knew.

So far, she'd managed to avoid getting into situations where she had to deal with someone who knew some of what was going on and might be inclined to want to know the rest, but unless business in Thrillers picked up a bit this afternoon, she and Indianna would have nothing to do but talk to one another. There was a chance that an exchange of intimate secrets might be on Indianna's agenda. She supposed that part of the problem was how much of a novice she still felt she was on the whole fetish scene. She knew that everyone said that nothing between consenting adults was out of order, but what people said and what they thought and what they did, and what they said behind your back, well that was maybe a different matter. And at the moment, at this delicious, tentative, terrifying, ecstatic stage of being utterly smitten and able to believe that her feelings were genuinely returned, she didn't want to share the details. The details were precious, that was all. Other people didn't need to know about any of it. She would just cradle her secrets close to herself, like the memories of the previous morning: the things the pair of them had said and done in that cramped shower cubicle, and the way she'd been screaming so loudly the fourth time she came that she'd needed a hand over her mouth so no one walking past the workshop thought there was a murder going on.

Cerise checked herself, and straightened up from where she'd been leaning against the wide wooden counter that ran most of the length of the shop.

'Cup of tea? I'm going to make one. Malorie said to help ourselves.'

It was a warm spring Friday, first real sunshine they'd had in weeks, and Cerise wasn't all that surprised that very few customers were coming through the door. Though clever use of screens and lighting, and lots of light-coloured wood and glass, made Thrillers look welcoming and bright rather than a gloomy cavern of depravity, the need to prevent the easily-offended from seeing too much of the stock meant there wasn't much natural daylight allowed in to the main shop floor. Thrillers sold fetishwear, kinky lingerie, boots, sex toys, restraints, erotic books and magazines and a hundred and one other things to do with pleasure and kink and, as such, probably wasn't going to be people's first port of call on a lovely, sunny day.

Cerise usually did secretarial or admin-based temping, her retail experience was fairly limited. Indianna, as far as Cerise knew, didn't have a regular job at present and that was why she had been the only other one able to respond to Ricky and Malorie's desperate Facebook pleas for a couple of warm bodies to come and mind the shop that afternoon while they, the couple who owned the place, went off to hunt down a supplier who had apparently gone bust without delivering the last order despite having been paid for it.

Cerise, a curvy girl with long black hair, had dithered a little about her clothing choices for the day. Working in a place like Thrillers had tempted her to go for full-on fetish, but the combination of hot weather, and the remembrance that neither Ricky nor Malorie had ever been attired in head-to-toe leather or latex when she'd visited the shop in the past, had prompted her to pick out a full-skirted dark green dress with a low neckline and cap sleeves. Indianna had also chosen to wear a dress: a simple, pale pink, sleeveless one which clung to her slim body and was short enough to show off her legs without being blatantly sexy. She had pinned up her light brown curls in a topknot, was wearing big hoop earrings and looked, Cerise thought, somehow corruptible.

Not that there was much chance of anyone corrupting anyone this afternoon. So far, they had sold a pair of bog-standard handcuffs and a bottle of massage oil to a softly-spoken man with huge thick-lensed glasses; an erotic novel; a t-shirt with a picture of a high-heeled boot; two boxes of latex gloves, and finally a pair of spike-heeled PVC boots to a woman who was dressed in standard middle-management nondescript clothing but who had the manner of an experienced dominatrix, all the same. But that had all been in the first hour and nothing had happened since. As neither of them were regular employees, they hadn't felt either the need or the entitlement to rearrange displays or do any stocktaking, and had fallen back on chatter and gossip, and all the while Cerise had felt that Indianna was leading up to something in particular, which she suspected would be The Question. They'd talked, a bit, about various people they knew and how those people interacted with one another. They'd discussed the whole concept of lifetime, lifestyle DS relationships, and Cerise had been a little relieved to hear that Indii wasn't terribly into that idea, either. Though she was a little younger than Cerise, the other girl had been on the scene for longer, and knew quite a few more people. There was some vague story, something slightly dodgy Indianna had been involved in a while back, wasn't there? Cerise remembered hearing a story, which Ricky and Malorie had been mixed up in as well, and hadn't that been something to do with a lifestyle male dom? She supposed that if Indii started asking too many nosy questions about Cerise's new relationship, Cerise could do some digging right back at her.

She shook her head, annoyed at herself. Indianna had never been anything but sweet and kind to her, and she was just being paranoid and self-obsessed.

'I think she mentioned something about chocolate Hob Nobs, as well,' she said to the younger girl. 'But it might have been: don't eat them all.'

Indianna giggled. 'We could pretend Ricky told us we could eat them,' she suggested. 'He might spank the pair of us. It's ages since I had a good seeing-to, and there's always been something about Ricky, really. I know he's a switch but there's that whole...' Then she dropped her gaze, and blushed.

'Shit, sorry. You're a top, really, aren't you?'

'Well, yeah, but don't stress.' Cerise almost blushed in her turn, hearing one of her beloved's favourite phrases on her own lips. Dizzy had sent her a message shortly after hearing that Cerise had told Ricky and Malorie she'd help them out: 'That's nice of you, darling girl, but have they specified whether they're paying cash, goods or sexual favours?' Malorie had, in fact, offered Cerise the choice between cash in hand, cash through the books or items from Thrillers up to the value of £50 at retail prices, and she'd opted for goods as there were a couple of designs she liked in the new range of fetish-themed sleeveless vests, and also a book of photography that she rather thought Dizzy would appreciate.

Indianna was looking at her a little oddly, and Cerise wondered if that was because the other girl had also noticed the catchphrase, or if it was purely because she'd drifted off into reveries again.

'Right, tea. And Hob Nobs, as well,' she announced. 'Don't sell everything while I'm in the kitchen.'

She heard the shop door open while she was waiting for the kettle to boil, but didn't think too much of it; Indianna was the more experienced of the pair of them anyway on the off-chance that the incoming customer wanted to discuss the suitability of different types of lube or buttplugs before making a purchase. However, when she returned to the shop floor, with mugs of tea, the sugar bowl and a saucer full of chocolate biscuits on a tin tray she'd found, Indianna was talking to an attractive sandy-haired man with a small goatee and the definite air of a hipster, and Indianna looked more than a little flustered. Cerise put the tray down on the counter and smiled an enquiring smile.

'Kyle Redmond,' the man said, holding out a hand to her, obviously expecting her name in return. She didn't offer it, though she did manage the handshake.

'He's from the TV company,' Indianna put in, and Cerise raised an eyebrow. Surely Ricky and Malorie would have said something, if they were having some cable guy round to convert them to Sky or whatever. Kyle Redmond, however, was clearly not going to let either of them stay uninformed.

'I did speak to someone last week about what we're doing with this programme,' he said. 'Though it wasn't either of you ladies. He just said I could drop in for a chat if I felt like it, and we could see how it went. We're looking at six distinct shows for the first series, each one covering a different aspect, so we've got swinging, pony-play, enforced chastity, full-time S and M relationships, the fashion and music aspect, and spanking.' As he said the last word, he stumbled a little over it, something which Cerise noted with interest. He recovered himself quickly and carried on: 'With a bit of luck we'll get a second series, and cover more topics, like bisexuality, rope bondage, paganism on the fetish scene.' He stopped, waiting for a reaction and Cerise imagined herself telling Dizzy all about it. Her lover was older than her, had been out and about on the scene for several years and had, more than once, expressed a rather jaundiced view of the type of programme Mr Redmond was talking about. Fetish recipes and kinky morris dancers any minute, Dizzy would have said.

'I'm not sure how we can help, really,' Indianna said, with what appeared to be genuine regret. 'Did you want to put up a poster or something, or leave us some flyers, so people who are interested can get in touch?'

~

Kyle was glad that the shop counter between him and the two girls was wide and sturdy, and that he could lean against it without seeming overfamiliar with them, or anything. He knew he was starting to get an erection, and even though his vintage check shirt hung over the outside of his trousers, he wasn't entirely sure they wouldn't notice if he stood up straight in front of them. The last couple of sessions of preliminary research he'd done had been interesting in that the people he talked to were serious enthusiasts and would come across well on camera, but they'd been either men or couples, and he hadn't, so far, found himself in a situation with two attractive women he was intending to ask about their experiences of spanking. He did have flyers in his messenger bag, and would happily leave a bundle on the counter, but gathering opinions on the spot was something he prided himself on being good at.

He shifted position slightly, hoping that his cock would subside, at least a little, and cleared his throat.

'That would be good, but could I just ask you a couple of questions? This is all off the record; I haven't got a camera crew with me, as you can see.' The taller one, whose gorgeous tits were flaunted the perfect amount in that 50s style dress, looked at him with a touch of amusement that sent a sharp little thrill to his groin. The other one, pretty in a fluffy sort of way that made him picture her giggling and kicking her legs while pinned down over someone's lap, gave a little shrug.

'I don't mind,' she said. 'As long as it's only a chat, OK?'

'Of course,' Kyle knew that he sounded truthful, probably because he was telling the truth. He couldn't film or record her without her permission and any insights she gave would only be used in the most generalised terms in the voiceover if she declined to participate in the programme itself. Miss Gorgeous Tits broke in for a moment to offer him a cup of tea, explaining that the kettle had not long boiled: when he accepted, she disappeared back to wherever she'd been before. He took a second to wonder whether this was because she'd decided it was safe to leave him and Miss Pink Minidress alone together, or whether she'd gone to summon that bloke he'd originally spoken to, for reinforcements. It probably didn't matter, either way.

He started with general questions: name, age, how long have you been into this sort of thing, what's special about spanking for you? Her answers were cheerful and relatively unselfconscious, though he thought he detected a slight unease about something in the background. Probably just the usual doubts about whether going public was a good idea or not, he supposed.

Indianna had already decided that she wasn't going to take part in this man's programme, but there wasn't any harm in talking to him. It might have been different if Kyle had been her type, if she'd been able to pick up any of the dominant vibe that tended to make her willing to go a step farther, but there wasn't a hint of it, none at all. If anything, she was detecting the opposite quality: buried some way down, but definitely there. She felt a sudden spark of mischief inside herself and opted to roll with it.

'It's the giving up to someone else, as much as what it actually feels like,' she told him. 'I get a bit, well, not exactly messed up sometimes but, if I've not done anything with anyone for a while, I really miss it.'

She noticed that Cerise had come back onto the shop floor with another mug of tea, but the other girl just set it quietly down near Kyle and backed away, clearly listening but not about to intrude. Indii glanced back at her, thinking once again that it was tricky when you wanted something from someone but weren't at all sure it would be on offer. The best thing to do would be to tell them a story and make it a good one.

'I got bitchy with the guy I was seeing,' she began. 'Not anything awful, it was all kind of understood. He's a top and we'd done a fair few things, but it had been more BDSM than CP, OK?'

Kyle nodded, but he didn't seem to be entirely sure, and it was Cerise who clarified things.

'BDSM's got a different feel, different style. You're talking about corporal punishment and that's, well, a lot more traditionalist in some ways.'

Indianna felt the first little prickle of arousal at the other woman's words. Cerise knew the score, all right. Indii had seen her in action more than once; doling out a thrashing by herself and, more recently, teaming up with Dizzy for what the pair of them called double-topping... And that was something Indii wasn't going to think about, right now.

'Anyway,' she said. 'I started winding him up, more playfully than really meaning it, but underneath I was, well, I could hardly wait for him to put his foot down, tell me I'd gone too far and was going to be punished. He knew bloody well what I wanted, but he was going to make me wait till he was ready.'

She gave a little wriggle, remembering the moment when Jim had said, all right, you little cow, you've really got this coming, and the dirty, dangerous smile he'd given her when he sat himself down on the edge of the bed and ordered her over his knee.

'I was wearing denim shorts, the really short kind, and he started with me still wearing them. He ran his hand over my bum, both where the shorts covered me, and then a bit lower down, onto my cheeks. The way I was lying, my shorts had hitched up a bit, so part of my bum was bare already. That was where the first smack landed, right on the bare, and I really yelled. "Oh, that won't do," he said. "You can take a lot more than that." But the next couple were over my shorts, and not quite as hard. He took it steady for a while, you know, kind of getting into a rhythm, and all the time he was telling me what a bad girl I was and how I was going to learn my lesson, and he had his other arm across my shoulders holding me down, and I felt...'

'How did it feel?' Kyle interrupted. He was staring at her with utter fascination, and his breathing seemed to have quickened. Indianna licked her lips; she'd put money on him having a hard on by now.

'Amazing,' she said. 'There was this wonderful, warm glow, spreading out from my arse, it was like it was going right through me. Then he kind of rolled up my shorts, pulled the legs of them up higher. I don't think he wanted to stop to take them off me. I remember one side ripped a bit while he was doing it. But then he started spanking me again, and it was harder this time, and it stung, but at the same time it felt even better. He had big hands, big strong hands, and it was like, whatever I did, I was safe and he'd look after me.'

She stopped, aware that she was juicing up at the memory. She wasn't sure how much more of it she wanted to share: could she tell this man that when she'd started moaning rather than squealing, Jim had ordered her to get up, take her shorts and her thong off and then he'd had her back down on his lap, given her six more really hard ones on the bare and stuck his fingers up her pussy and frigged her till she nearly lost her mind. Dropping her gaze to the counter, she hoped she wasn't going totally red in the face.

'So, just a hand-spanking,' Kyle said, his voice almost cracking. 'How do you feel about, you know, hairbrushes? Or canes? Do you like being... Being hit with them, too? Or have you never tried it?'

Cerise had been managing to keep quiet for most of this conversation, though she was pretty sure that she was going to have to intervene at some point. Perhaps the feeling of protectiveness she was developing towards Indii was one of those side-effects of becoming a better dominant, perhaps it was just the way people generally tended to react to the other girl's looks and demeanour. Either way, she knew she'd read this TV researcher right. And, just like that, she knew what she was going to do about it.

'How many of them have you tried, though, Kyle?' she asked, and when he jumped and half-turned to gaze at her with a full-on bunny-in-the-headlights expression, she almost laughed. She was aware of her own voice taking on that slightly more upmarket, autocratic tone she liked to use during scenes.

'Don't you think your research would be better if you introduced a practical element to it? Even if it's only a hand-spanking, you ought to give it a try.'

He might have flounced out, at that point, or blandly diverted the discussion, or made it clear in some other way that no, no chance, nobody was getting anywhere near his backside, but Cerise was pretty sure that a stiff prick has, as they say, no conscience and will override common sense. He straightened up, slowly, and when she took a deliberate look at the front of his body, he flushed a little and she saw, as she'd expected, a bulge in his clothing, detectable even under the below-waist-level shirt. There was a pause, during which he was obviously struggling with the conflict between his professional role and his libido, and then he hung his head.

'Yeah. Yes. Um, yes, Miss. Is that right?'

'What are you going to use, Cerise?' Indianna said, eagerly. 'Do you want the demo kit?'

Demo kit? Cerise was nearly thrown out of the moment before she remembered that Malorie and Ricky had shown the pair of them a box full of common implements that customers were allowed to try out, on the proviso that they only did so on clothed bodies and any breakages were paid for.

'I'll just use my hand, thanks. But you'd better go and lock the door,' she said, and made her way to the sturdy, old-fashioned wooden chair that stood outside Thrillers' changing rooms. She moved it into a more central position and sat down, keeping her eyes on Kyle all the time.

'Come along, then. Over my knee.'

~

Kyle hadn't come in his pants for nearly a decade, but he wouldn't be surprised if it happened again in the next few minutes. His legs felt slightly shaky as he crossed the floor to the woman who sat there waiting for him, her face calmly amused, and a look of utter authority in her eyes. His cock was so hard it almost hurt.

He was tall enough to brace his hands on the floor as he positioned himself. She hadn't told him to remove his trousers or anything, and he asked himself whether he would have complied if she had. She did take hold of the bottom of his shirt and tuck it up out of the way, once he was in place, but that was all. He was aware of her hand running all over his arse, lightly at first, then pressing down a little, giving each cheek a squeeze. The anticipation of the first blow was both exciting and terrifying, and he knew she was prolonging it on purpose. She lifted her hand, he closed his eyes, and then it happened.

Smack!

The sound seemed astonishingly loud, and even through his trousers and boxers he could feel the impact. He let out a little gasp, and then she did it again. Right from the beginning, she was spreading the blows evenly over his buttocks; the left, the right, the crown of his rump, the tender place just below the curve of each cheek. They weren't horribly painful, though the stinging effect began to accumulate quite quickly. She paused for a moment, after what felt like several dozen spanks, and started rubbing and stroking his arse through his pants again.

'Warming up nicely,' she said. 'So how does it feel?'

'I bet he's good and red,' he heard the other girl say – she'd told him her name, hadn't she? Indianna, that was it.

'I think you should get his pants down and have a look,' she added and Kyle thought: well, thanks, Indianna.

'Yes, we should,' his punisher agreed. 'Stand up and drop those trousers. Keep your underpants on, mind.'

Kyle did as she asked, grateful for the small concession of being allowed to keep his boxers on. It wasn't that he thought they would provide that much protection from her firm and purposeful hand, it was more that he suspected his excited prick was beginning to leak slow drops of clear fluid from its swollen, throbbing tip. The pants would cover that much, with any luck.

Back over her thighs again, he managed to keep the front of his shirt over his boxers as well, even as she rolled up the back of it. His buttocks felt amazingly warm, with a hot, tingly sensation radiating from them. He heard Miss – as he now thought of her – call Indianna closer to inspect the redness, pulling the boxer shorts up high to show it off as she did so. She pulled them right up the crack of his arse, and something about the way the strip of fabric pressed on his perineum and anus made him struggle not to groan aloud. Down came her hand again, on a now-bared cheek, and again on the other, and again, and again, and again. The impact was sharper, considerably so, but still made him feel a lot more excitement than pain. She carried on for quite some time, and he closed his eyes, surrendering to the sensations.

'Enough,' she said, at last. 'My hand's getting sore.'

He moaned. He'd become aware, in the last few moments, that he was actually very close to shooting his load, and while part of him longed to let it all go, let his cock explode in his pants, another part of him worried that she'd freak out, that he'd be totally overstepping the mark if he did something like that.

'Stand up. Hands on your head,' she ordered him, and he complied, struggling to keep himself under control.

'Look at the state of him,' Indianna teased, and Kyle found himself enjoying the shame that washed over him. 'He looks like his dick's about to rip a hole in his pants.'

'Do you want to help him out with it?' Miss had the air of someone granting a massive favour, but whether Kyle or Indianna was the one getting the reward, he wasn't quite sure. Indianna didn't answer in words, simply came up beside him, put her hand inside his already-dampened boxers and wrapped her fingers round his aching, straining tool. She only had to squeeze, and slide, and gently tug for a moment or two before he found himself shouting something, thrusting his hips against the air and spraying jet after boiling jet of spunk over her hand and into his pants. He staggered back against the door of the changing room, only just managing to stay on his feet.

'Is that... is it always like that?' he managed to ask, a few seconds later. Indianna and her friend, or boss, or mistress, or whatever she was, simply grinned at him.

'Maybe,' they said, almost in unison.

~

Once they'd sent Kyle on his way, with a glowing arse and an air of dazed revelation, they turned the sign on the door back to Open, and checked there were no visible indications of what had happened. Cerise sent Indii back to the kitchen for a round of teas to replace the ones they hadn't got around to drinking, reckoning it was the other girl's turn. Her left palm throbbed slightly, but it wasn't too bad and certainly it would be nothing compared to how Mr TV Guy was going to feel when the aftershocks of his orgasm started wearing off.

Indianna came back and put the mugs on the counter.

'Cerise, I really wanted to ask you, about doing stuff with...' she began, and Cerise took a deep breath. Here was The Question, after all. Oh, why not just get it out of the way.

'Yes, I like boys, I like girls, and I like Dizzy. And we're seeing one another, not just doing men in clubs. Yes. OK?'

Indianna's eyes opened wide.

'Oh shit, I wasn't being, you know, having a go. I heard about you and Dizzy and I think it's brilliant, Malorie told me she'd never seen Dizzy so happy in years. But the girls and boys thing – I've only ever seen the two of you do male subs.'

'Yes?'

Indianna fidgeted. 'You spanked that guy. It was really horny. I thought – I wondered.'

'I see.' Cerise made a rather ostentatious display of looking at her watch.

'Well, it's ten past five, and those two said they wouldn't be back till after closing time. So if you can control yourself for another twenty minutes, then I'll give you exactly what you deserve. Is that all right with you, missy? We might at least get our teas drunk, this time.'

With a naughty giggle, Indianna agreed and Cerise, sipping tea, reflected that she would have plenty to tell her beloved when they met up later that night. Including the fact that everyone else was happy for the two of them, as well.

THE TASTE OF
BLACKBERRIES

There had been a little talk, earlier in the evening, about the idea that the perfect dominant always had the sub under absolute control; predictably, Malorie had been the first one to call bullshit. Natasha thought her friend might have been slightly disappointed that no one actually thought it either possible or desirable to carry erotic power exchange quite that far, and Malorie's partner, Ricky, had told her she could go and have that fight online some time but she wasn't going to get it tonight.

As the guest on that particular night who was the most into roleplay, Madame Natasha had wondered if anyone was going to have a dig at her, or at her maid, Esmeralda, but the subject had changed fairly swiftly to the possibilities of running another fetish night at the Seven Stars and whether it would be a regular one, and who should actually be in charge of it. The party had continued in its usual enjoyable fashion – one of Master Mike's smaller gatherings, but still about twenty guests there, so more than enough opportunity to have some fun, catch up on some gossip and generally please yourself however you chose. Esmeralda, as was always the case at social events, was in and out of the different rooms, refilling glasses, dealing with any spillages, offering nibbles, or down in the kitchen washing up.

Natasha didn't consider this a demonstration of total control. Esmeralda loved being a maid, and part of her enjoyment came from doing traditional maid-type things – but another part of the enjoyment, for both maid and mistress, lay in the rules being broken. Often, at a house party, Esmeralda would be cheeky to another guest, or disobey an order, and it was understood that any such transgressions should be reported to Natasha straight away, so that she could punish the naughty, rebellious maid. Sometimes, of course, Natasha would decline to administer punishment herself, and invite whoever considered themselves disrespected to apply a whip, or a cane, or a paddle to Esmeralda's backside.

As there had been some people at Mike's who Natasha hadn't seen for several months, she'd found herself absorbed in a long catch-up session, and it was only towards the end of the night that she realised she hadn't once been alerted to any misbehaviour on Esmeralda's part. Extracting herself from a conversation about online censorship, she went in search of the maid, and found Esmeralda in the otherwise-deserted kitchen, washing glasses and plates with concentrated determination.

'Well, girl,' she said, and stopped. It was rare for Madame Natasha to be lost for words, but something about Esmeralda's stance confounded her.

'Just finishing the washing up, ma'am,' Esmeralda muttered, without turning round.

Natasha waited, but nothing else was forthcoming. She knew perfectly well that she had done nothing to hurt the maid's feelings – the two of them knew each other thoroughly enough for her to be sure of that. Something was clearly very wrong, though, and Natasha decided that she wasn't going to get to the bottom of it at the party.

'It's about time we were leaving,' she said. 'Finish those glasses and call for a taxi while I go and say goodnight.'

~

There were a couple of cab firms they usually used, who could be trusted to send drivers who wouldn't gawp or freak or make insulting remarks, though both of them had previously agreed that, in the case of having to use another company, they would fall back on 'fancy dress party' as an explanation for their attire. As it was, tonight they got the chubby old bloke who never said anything apart from 'Where to?' and 'That'll be twenty quid, please.' All through the journey, Natasha was more and more aware that something was wrong, and she struggled to work out what it might be. Surely Esmeralda hadn't been hurt by Malorie banging on about true BDSM relationships: seriously unlikely, as Esmeralda had known Malorie nearly as long as Natasha.

Eventually, they were back at Natasha's place, going in elegantly through the door, mistress and maid, up the stairs and safely home, and then Esmeralda was taking a deep breath and saying, 'Madame, would it be possible for the maid to take a holiday and go home tonight?'

Natasha looked at the maid, and then she looked, as she sometimes did, through the maid. This was going to be one of those times. 'Talk to me,' she said, and hoped, very hard, that it wasn't going to be Esmeralda who answered.

'Nat, love, I'm sorry, it's nothing about you, 'said the person in front of her, and Natasha said, 'Les, come and sit down and have a drink, and tell me what the problem is.'

Though it was generally something like a rule that Esmeralda was the maid when she was wearing a maid's uniform, and Les the man who arrived and departed from Natasha's flat in unremarkable male clothing, the line could sometimes blur without ruining the game for either of them. So Natasha was the one who made two mugs of hot chocolate and spiked them with Cointreau, while her longterm companion sat on the sofa, still in Esmeralda's black satin dress and frilly white apron, but with the maid's cap and the new blonde wig removed. Natasha did spare a moment to be glad that she'd opted for her dark green latex jacket and matching flared skirt tonight rather than a corset; the green outfit was not too uncomfortable to keep on if this turned out to be a long discussion.

When they were comfortably settled in front of the fake log fire, she said, again, 'Talk to me. What's the matter?'

Esmeralda/Les gave a long sigh and gulped some of the contents of the mug.

'I'm really sorry, Nat. Like I said, it's not about you, or about us, it's just... I heard about Miss Adelaide tonight, and it's hit me harder than I thought it would.'

Natasha controlled her first reaction, which was sheer bewilderment, and said, 'Miss Adelaide? Hang on, I remember someone saying something, a couple of months back. But I didn't know you knew her.'

'Oh, not well. I haven't – I mean, I hadn't actually seen her for nearly ten years. I heard she wasn't well, and I meant to get in touch at some point, but then that Charles, the one with the big beard, he was talking to his girlfriend and said something about going to Miss Adelaide's funeral a few months ago.'

'I think Mike went, as well,' Natasha said. 'He mentioned it at the time. Oh, shit, I wish I'd told you, now. It just didn't occur to me that you knew her.'

She put an arm round her slave, something that rarely happened. 'I'm really sorry. Honestly.'

The hug was reciprocated, and Natasha was glad. At the bottom of the mistress-and-slave relationship, there was a deep and longstanding friendship between them. Both were aware that the other had history, had been involved with other people and, certainly in Natasha's case, had occasional and ongoing sexual relationships with other people, but they rarely discussed it.

'Do you want to tell me about it?' Natasha asked. 'You don't have to, but it's fine if you want to.' It crossed her mind that a more appropriate response, at least in some people's eyes, might have been to bend the maid over and give her a good beating to reaffirm her role and take her mind off her troubles, but she was fairly sure that this wasn't what was required, tonight. Listening was what her dear friend needed her to do.

'Well, Miss Adelaide was one of my first. I suppose you could say she was the first one that really mattered,' said Les. 'Even though it was only the one day, really.'

Natasha sat back, picked up her mug and said, 'Go on.'

'I was just another fairly new male sub, at that point, but I caught her eye, or she caught mine, or something. We got talking in a club one night and she asked me what sort of thing I was into. I told her some of my fantasies, and she said, you should come and see me. Next week. We swapped phone numbers, and I dithered a bit, because I wasn't sure she meant it, but then I did go.

It was late summer, end of August, and it was a warm sunny day. I drove over there, with a bag of gear on the back seat, just wearing jeans and a t-shirt, feeling nervous and seriously excited, all at the same time. She lived in one of these big Victorian detached places, with a massive back garden that had loads of trees at the end of it, and a big fence either side. Her maid answered the door, in full maid costume – apron, cap, plain black dress, and I remember being a bit thrilled by that, and then wondering if the maid answered the door like that to everyone. Miss Adelaide was sitting on the sofa, in front of the big window that gave a view over the garden. She was wearing a black corset over a sheer black blouse, and a long red silk skirt, and drinking tea. She told me to sit down, offered me a cup of tea and when I said no, thanks, she sent the maid away. We had a proper little chat – boundaries and limits and what I was expecting and all that – and then she said, when I snap my fingers, it begins. Your safeword is Rosebud.'

'So, then she snapped her fingers?' Natasha said, when the silence seemed to stretch out a little too long.

'Oh yes. She finished her tea, put down her cup, snapped her fingers and said, strip. Everything off, right now. And when you're naked, kneel at my feet. So I did what she said, and she sat there, watching me, absolutely still, like she was posing for a portrait artist. She must have been at least sixty then, but she was beautiful. She wasn't very big, but so much presence. So much personality. I was kneeling at her feet, completely naked, for ages before she did anything, but the atmosphere in the room was amazing. I'd been excited on the way over, and even more once I was actually in the room with her, so I wasn't that surprised that I got an erection. It was really obvious, because I was naked, and I was worried about it. I wasn't sure she'd approve. Then she reached over, picked up the teacup and put it on the floor in front of me.

'Ejaculate into that,' she said. 'And then we'll continue. You won't be in the correct frame of mind until you have dealt with yourself.'

I was still fairly inexperienced, and the whole thing was so incredible that I thought I might not be able to, you know, perform. But at the same time, I was aroused, more than ever. So I did what she said, I played with myself in front of her and I shot my load into that cup. And then she ordered me to drink it.'

Natasha had forgotten all about her hot chocolate; she was enthralled by the story.

'Go on,' she said.

'She picked up this little silver bell and rang it, and the maid came back. Miss Adelaide told her to take me to the kitchen and put me to work. I started to get up and she said. No. You crawl. You crawl on your hands and knees. So that's what I did. I crawled all the way to the kitchen, and the maid gave me a bucket and a scrubbing brush and made me scrub the floor. It was clean already, I remember, but I knew better than to say so. I got on and scrubbed, and the maid was doing things like peeling potatoes and flicking through recipe books, and she and Miss Adelaide were chattering about what to have for dinner. Then the maid got a bottle of olive oil out of a cupboard and dropped it on the floor that I'd just been cleaning. I honestly think it was an accident, though I'm not completely sure. I do know the idea wasn't to get me into trouble. I think the maid just liked to have an 'accident' from time to time, because of the consequences.

Miss Adelaide told her to bend over the table and pull up her skirt. She had on a white, frilly petticoat underneath, with a proper, old-fashioned suspender belt, thick black stockings and plain black panties. Miss Adelaide got a wooden spoon out of a drawer and said, six for carelessness. She hit pretty hard; I heard every single one and I almost felt them. It was over the panties, not on the bare, but it must have been pretty harsh, all the same. The maid didn't scream or anything, just said, One, thank you mistress, two, thank you mistress, till she'd had all six. Then, when it was over, she stood up and pulled down her petticoat and skirt. She did a little curtsey and went back to the cupboard. Neither she nor Miss Adelaide had paid me any attention while the maid was getting a beating, but then Miss Adelaide turned round to me and said, stop staring and clean up that mess. I won't have any slacking from either of you. She went out of the room, and the maid gave me some kitchen roll so I could mop up the oil more easily. I don't think the maid spoke more than a couple of sentences to me the whole time I was there.

Miss Adelaide came back in just as I'd finished with the oil spill, and she had a little black paddle in her hand. Now it was my turn to bend over the table – I should have been getting on with my work rather than watching the maid take a punishment. She laid that paddle on good and hard. It wasn't very big but it was seriously stingy, and my bottom felt like it was on fire by the time she'd finished, but my head was almost floating. It was like I'd gone into a completely different world, from the minute Miss Adelaide had snapped her fingers.

After that, she had me out in the garden, still naked. I honestly don't know if she had some kind of understanding with her neighbours or if she just knew exactly when they were in or out of their houses, because even with the fences and the trees, I would have thought anyone looking out of an upstairs window would have been able to see what was going on. I suppose some people might have been freaked out at the idea, but I was younger then and it didn't bother me in the least. This was before the time when you might have worried that someone would take a picture of you and put it on Facebook or Youtube and it would be all round the world in about ten minutes, anyway.

I was made to do various garden chores: weeding, and pruning the rosebushes, that type of thing. I'm not exactly an expert, but I think she knew that, she didn't have me doing anything too complicated. She sat on a wooden bench, watching me, and the maid came in and out a couple of times. It was very hot, and when I was bending over, I could really feel the sun on my well-thrashed arse. It's hard to describe what was going on in my head. Everything was unreal, but I was happy. And then she said, that's enough. The maid had come out again, and was carrying a bowl. I wondered what was in it, and then, when the two of them came over to the edge of the flower bed, I saw the bowl was empty. There was also a little bag that she must have given to her mistress, because Miss Adelaide was carrying that.

'Come along,' Miss Adelaide said. They walked down the garden, and I followed them, on my hands and knees. Like I said, it was a big garden, and it seemed to back on to a park, or maybe it was a golf course or something, because there was a fence at the end of it, and loads of trees behind the fence. And all over the fence and growing round it, there were brambles, a huge mass of them. And they were full of blackberries, most of which were ripe. I remember one side of the garden was quite shady, and the other was still getting the full impact of the sun. It was the shady corner that the maid got sent to, and I understood that she was simply going to pick the blackberries. I thought Miss Adelaide had something different in mind for me, and I waited for her to tell me what it was.

She told me to stand up, and then she put her bag on the floor, opened it and took out a pair of gloves. They were the sort of thick, heavy ones you use for gardening, we're not talking elegant black leather. She got me to go backwards, slowly, until I was practically touching the big bramble tangle in the corner, and then she said, stand very, very still. The other thing she had taken out of her bag was a card strip with several big bulldog clips on it. That was when I found out what the gloves were for. She went in among the brambles and got hold of some of the long, springy cables, and twined them round my arms, and round my legs, not tightly, but close enough to touch. She used the bulldog clips to hold them in place. I don't know if you know, but even the leaves of brambles have prickles on them, just tiny little ones, but you can definitely feel them.

'Stand very, very still,' she said again, once she'd finished winding the things round me. I did as I was told. None of the thorns were actually digging on, but I was aware they were there, and that if I wriggled or moved or tried to get away, I'd be seriously scratched.

'The counterbalance of pleasure and pain,' Miss Adelaide said, very softly. 'I love to explore it. I love to demonstrate it. Now, let's see what that girl's been doing.'

She went off towards the other side of the garden. I didn't even dare to turn my head in case I scratched myself, so I just stood there, waiting. I don't know how long it was, but it can't have been many minutes – the garden was big, but we're not talking Hyde Park here. Then the two of them came back; Miss Adelaide and the maid. The maid had filled the bowl with blackberries.

You remember I said at the beginning, when she made me come into her teacup, and I thought for a minute I'd lose my hard on?'

Natasha jumped slightly: so captivated by what she was hearing that she had almost imagined herself right there, in that sunny garden, watching the naked figure trapped and tormented by the thorny bramble cables.

'Uh, yeah,' she managed. 'But that's just it, isn't it? Some people would be scared and upset, other people

– well, like you, love – they enjoy it even more when it's scary.'

'Yes, that's true. So I was hard again when they got back to me. Partly because I was pretty sure something interesting was coming up, partly because I was so turned on at the thought of being completely helpless. I'd surrendered myself totally to Miss Adelaide and she could do anything she wanted. It was frightening, and almost frustrating, because I wanted to touch myself, but obviously I couldn't move. Miss Adelaide looked at my cock, pointing up at the sky, and she said to the maid, 'I believe that's your next task, girl.'

She took the bowl of fruit from the maid and came to stand beside me, right up close to me, while the maid got down on her knees.

'Open your mouth,' Miss Adelaide said, and then laughed, I'll never forget that laugh. Someone else once said she was like a dark goddess, but that's not really it. I think of that old poem we learned at school, the Belle Dame Sans Merci, the queen of the fairies. 'Both of you,' she said, and laughed again. 'Both of you open your mouths. You've both earned something sweet.'

So the maid began to suck my cock, and I thought for one mad minute that Miss Adelaide was expecting me to perform oral service on her, and I couldn't imagine how I was going to do it without tearing myself to pieces. But no, that wasn't what she meant.

It was the berries. She fed me a ripe one and told me to crush it against the roof of my mouth with my tongue and taste the juice of it. And then she gave me another, and another. They were the best blackberries I ever tasted, just at that pitch of ripeness before they turn, and I wanted to go on eating them, but more than half my mind was also on my cock, and the feel of the maid's lips and sharp little teeth working on me. I closed my eyes, and the sun burned down on my eyelids, and Miss Adelaide had one hand pressed against the small of my back and she said, one more time, 'Be very, very still,' and then I came in the maid's mouth, and I felt the thorns dig into me in half a dozen places, and when I screamed there was blackberry juice running down my chin.'

Natasha sat in silence as Les concluded his story: how Miss Adelaide and the maid had carefully freed him from his bramble bondage and the maid had taken him back to the house for a shower and a dab or two of antiseptic on the scratches he hadn't been able to avoid inflicting on himself. It was definitely Les speaking and had been from the beginning. She was quite glad she hadn't turned on the main light, though: Les's everyday, conversational voice and Esmeralda's appearance would always be slightly at odds.

'Did you see her again, after that? I mean, did you stay with her?' she asked.

Les sighed. 'I went back a few more times. She liked to have a few houseboys, as she put it, but after a while I started getting more and more envious of the maid. I wanted to be the one in the dress and pinny, doing the kitchen work and ordering the houseboys around. But Miss Adelaide's maid lived with her, they were a couple, and she didn't want anyone else doing that sort of thing for her mistress. So Miss Adelaide put me on to the Duchess, who ran a maid-training academy. I think I told you I went there, didn't I?

'Yes, you did.' Natasha was glad to find herself back on familiar ground. 'I met the Duchess about three years ago, she's lovely.'

It was fine, now, it was all going to be fine. Telling the story had soothed Les/Esmeralda, in the way that talking about someone you have lost often does. For a moment, the two of them clasped each other's hands, and then they smiled at each other, and drew calmly apart. The maid got to her feet and collected the mugs.

'I'll wash these up before bedtime. Ma'am,' said Esmeralda, with the slightest hint of a curtsey, and Natasha stretched and got to her feet. It would be a while until blackberries were in season again, but she thought there were probably one or two isolated places she might be able to find some, when the time was right.

LOVE THE CHARACTERS?

READ BLACK HEART
BY ZAK JANE KEIR

Rosa has put her kinky days behind her, and built a new life as the landlady of a popular pub, but the past isn't easily forgotten. It seems like her beautiful barman, Daniel, really needs a strict Mistress to take him in hand, and it's Rosa he has a deep, submissive crush on.

Natasha, Rosa's new best friend, wants to help her rediscover her inner dominatrix, particularly now that legendary fetish club The Scarlet House is about to relaunch.

But Rosa's previous adventures on the scene ended badly, and Daniel's relationship with the drummer in his band is closer than he's letting on. Maybe everyone's got a dirty little secret, deep inside...

PRAISE FOR BLACK HEART

"A far better, more compelling read than the majority of erotica. You feel you are there right from the start, with descriptions of people and places that echo the world of fetish and BDSM as it really is."

"The sex and fetish scenes are extremely sexy and obviously written from a very knowledgeable point of view."

Find out more:
https://amzn.to/2JNA210

Printed in Great Britain
by Amazon